Troublesome Creek

Wesley Mullins

Cover Design: Ron Logan

PRAISE FOR TROUBLESOME CREEK

"The characters really 'leap off the page' and capture the spirit of this fictitious Appalachian community."
- Fade In Magazine

Awards from Film Festivals and Screenwriting Competitions:

- First Prize – Fade In Magazine
- First Prize – San Pedro International Film Festival
- First Prize – Illinois International Film Festival
- First Prize – West Field Screenwriting Awards

Ranked in the top ten percent of 2019 Academy Award Nicholl Submissions.

© 2019 Academy of Motion Picture Arts and Sciences

Performed on stage:
- Omaha International Film Festival
- Harlem International Film Festival

Officially recognized in over two dozen competitions and festivals.

Troublesome Creek

Dedication: For My Grandparents

They got up early. Real early. They milked cows and ploughed land and birthed babies and plucked chickens and slaughtered pigs and made their own clothes.

And they did dozens of other things I can't do today so they could survive in the world they knew.

Troublesome Creek

Troublesome Creek

CHAPTER 1

Jerry led his nephew through the shadows of the tall
white oaks and red maples of the Daniel Boone
National Forest. They walked along an elk trail,
stepping on leaves still holding rain from the previous
morning.

"Ouch," his nephew, Andrew, said as he pulled
blackberry thorns from his arm, tiny drops of blood
filling the holes in his skin.

"You gotta watch them berries, Andrew."

Even though he was off duty and in plain clothes,
thirty-nine-year-old Jerry Somerset still wore a gun on
his hip. With his short military cut, wiry build and
medium height, Jerry looked like he could be on leave
from the army. A staff sergeant maybe. Andrew,
twenty-one, wore dark jeans and a concert t-shirt of a
band from Portland he followed online. He intended to
see them the following summer when they planned to
travel east. Andrew's shoulder-length greasy hair hung
below his black knit cap and curled at the ends. He
wore boots, but not the kind of boots Jerry said belong

in the woods.

"This is another one of them chestnuts," said Jerry, stopping to inspect a broken seedling. "I swear," he added, disgusted.

Andrew did not respond. He looked to his uncle.

Jerry continued, "Years ago, chestnuts were the most common tree in these hills. But some blight came over from Japan and plum near wiped them all out."

"That what got this one? A blight?"

"No, that blight aint around no more. This was broken down by an elk. See here?" Jerry pointed to a fatal bend in the young tree's base.

"A big one at that." Jerry motioned to a choppy trail of heavy elk tracks that meandered down the mountain, crossing over rocks and plowing through small black gum trees. "That elk don't realize if they'd just let these trees grow up, they'd produce nuts for everybody. For them, for the squirrels. Everybody."

Andrew tried to straighten the little tree and return it to an upright position. With his small hands and what his classmates used to call "girl's wrists," he steadied the sapling. When he pulled his hands away, it collapsed.

"By killing them when they're young," Jerry continued, "they'll never produce nothing."

The two proceeded through the dark forest. Although a sizzling July morning, with the sun already warming the yards and homes of people throughout Eastern Kentucky, Jerry and Andrew stayed cool along the canopied trail, as the mountains and trees worked together to inform the sun it was not welcome.

Somewhere, an engine rumbled. Jerry stopped and extended his hand. "Hear that? Not supposed to have four-wheelers back here."

"You aint no game warden," said Andrew. "What do

you care?"

"Law's law, Andrew."

Jerry and Andrew passed between two slabs of shale the size of Volkswagens. Jagged-edged and moss-covered, the rocks provided a corridor up the hill, toward the sound of the engine. On the other side, they saw a hunter green ATV buggy. A shiny piece of machinery that looked like it had just rolled off the assembly line. Leather seats, optional winch package, all the fixings. Jerry recognized its owner.

"It's Big Dan," he said.

Big Dan Calhoun, not a large man physically but one who made every room he was in seem small, was out of the ATV, inspecting the area. In his sixties, Big Dan wore a Silver Belly Stetson and a pair of Larry Mahan ostrich-skin boots. Jerry would have also said those boots did not belong in the woods, but Big Dan's pair stayed clean and scuff-free, as if he walked through life slightly elevated.

"Big Dan!" Jerry called to him.

"Jerry, you never know who you'll find in Daniel Boone's forest," Big Dan replied.

Jerry and Andrew approached. "You know my nephew, Andrew?" asked Jerry.

"Seen him around, but never met him," said Big Dan. "What do ya say, young fella?"

"Hello."

"I was just telling Andrew that ATVs aint allowed back here. This is the protected part of the forest. Foot traffic only. You know that, right?"

Big Dan turned around and united his hands behind his back to mimic being handcuffed. "Well, you caught me, Jerry," said Big Dan. "I want my lawyer, a phone call and three hots and a cot."

Jerry shook his head, ashamed that Andrew saw his authority mocked. Big Dan looked over his shoulder, noticed Jerry's defeat and grinned at him. He turned around and smacked Jerry on the back.

"Of course, I know your boss pretty well," Big Dan said, chuckling. "And he probably wouldn't want you arresting his old man. Am I right?"

Jerry ignored the question. He looked inside the ATV. "This is a nice machine here. That's for sure."

"You know, we could probably get a good deal on a couple for you and Danny. For the department, of course. Say it's for hunting pot growers and tracking outlaws through the hills."

"Outlaws through the hills," Jerry repeated. "I like the sound of that."

"Yessir. You and Danny would be like two of them old rangers from long ago down in Texas, hunting bandits on horseback. Except you'd be riding in style."

Jerry studied the surroundings. "You know, I can only think of one reason why you'd be back here like this."

"And what reason's that?"

"Scouting. You aint planning on hunting this season in the protected area, are you?"

Big Dan thought about the question. He sized up Jerry and his resolve. "Would that be a problem?"

The left corner of Big Dan's mouth betrayed him, twitching slightly to expose his guilt. Jerry again shook his head in defeat.

"We gotta get these elk," Big Dan said. "There's too many of them. They're destroying everything."

"They are out of control," said Jerry. "I agree with you there. We got a call the other day from Robert Burchell. Said his whole corn crop this year was wiped

4

out by a herd. There one day, all tasseled up and ready to silk, and then gone the next morning. Looked like a row of tanks had invaded his garden."

"And it aint the elk's fault, Jerry. They're just doing what they're supposed to do," said Big Dan, eagerly. "We've put them in a position where they don't have any good options. If you give an elk, or a man for that matter, only bad options, he'll only make bad choices."

Jerry sighed. "Too many of them, huh?"

"Yep."

"I aint gonna argue that, but this is federal land and federal law. Heck, you could get the FBI down here over something like that."

Big Dan paused and looked out over the mountains. He breathed in the wet, morning air and saw the fog still clinging to the thick needles of the pines and the welcoming arms of the giant sycamores. "Them old boys aint gonna scare Big Dan," he said. "Not here, they won't."

"I guess not, but I'll check out here when hunting season opens. You better not be here. This aint no joke."

Big Dan looked over to Andrew and shrugged his shoulders as if to say, "Maybe. I'll try."

*   *   *

Out of a cooler in the back of his car, Jerry retrieved two bottles of Ale-8. He opened one and handed it to Andrew.

"Oh, I didn't know you brought these," Andrew said and took a sip from the bottle.

Jerry opened the other and took a long drink, the citrus and ginger fizz building in his stomach before

5

erupting in a long, steady belch. "Look, I know I said law's law. You're right. And that's the truth, Andrew. But there are laws for families like ours, and then there's laws for families like Big Dan's. Just aint no way around something like that."

Jerry took another long slug from his soft drink. "If I finish mine before yours is half gone," he said, "I'm taking yours too."

Andrew smiled. He turned up his bottle and raced with his uncle.

Jerry had pretended his invitation to Andrew this morning to join him on his walk in the woods was spontaneous, but it was not. Jerry's mother, Mary, had mentioned concerns to him she had about her grandson, the young man who had lived with her most of his life. Andrew's mother also had a bedroom in the house where she was raised, but the duties of raising the troubled boy more often fell to Mary and Jerry.

Recently, Mary saw her grandson had become more withdrawn, quiet and mysterious. More than two years had elapsed since Andrew's last incident, but Mary did not want to see him again behind bars. He landed there after an arrest for stealing items from their home. Items he sold to buy Xanax and Vicodin. Mary filed a police report that her house had been robbed, but when one of Jerry's fellow deputies tracked one of the items back to a pawnshop, the owner confirmed they were brought to his business by Andrew Somerset. Or Andrew Eldridge, if he was using the last name of his father. He sometimes did that to remind his mother of the man who left her when Andrew was three years old.

Asking Jerry to spend more time with her grandson was part of Mary's overall plan that also included seeking help from Preacher Bryant. The Baptist minister suggested Andrew attend his weekly group recovery program, where treating the soul was the first step to addiction healing. Preacher Bryant also suggested Andrew develop a hobby, something other than playing video games, where he physically engaged with God's world.

"Done," Jerry said, holding up his empty Ale-8 bottle.

Andrew smiled. "I wasn't trying. Don't want to waste mine."

"Well, aren't you clever," said Jerry. "I believe Mom's warming up that roast she made Sunday. We should head home. That'll make some mighty good sandwiches."

Andrew shook his head in agreement and began toward the car. Jerry stepped to the driver's door and looked over to his nephew. He saw Andrew's smile disappear once he no longer thought his uncle was watching. The cheer and excitement that Jerry had seen moments earlier was replaced by a blank, emotionless gaze. Jerry sometimes saw this look on Andrew, and it scared him. Jerry saw this face of disinterest before on people who sat in the back of his patrol car. The kind of people who did not resist or complain, would not yell at him about his choice of profession or threaten him with lawsuits. They did not proclaim their innocence or struggle to free themselves in any way. They just sat in his car and accepted it.

*   *   *

In the bedroom of his trailer, Jerry stripped to a t-shirt and boxer shorts. His thirty-three-year-old wife, Susie, was already in bed with her eyes closed. Jerry talked as he prepared to join her. "He seemed pretty interested when I was talking to him about some chestnut trees we found."

Susie opened one eye and smiled. "If that boy ever gets his life together, it will all be because of his Uncle Jerry. That's for sure."

"Well, Mom helps too."

"Oh, don't get me started. She don't see no wrong in anything he does." Susie sat up in bed. At over eight months pregnant, she had to use her elbows to walk her back and shoulders up the headboard. "And that's the worst way you can be with someone with problems like his."

"Oh yeah?" Jerry asked.

"Uh-huh."

"When did you get so smart?" said Jerry, getting into bed. He reached over and placed his hand on her stomach. "How's this little one today?"

"She moved a bunch of times. I had the TV on and was watching them do a makeover of this old rundown house, on a lake somewhere in Mississippi."

"A lake house?"

"Yeah. When they showed the new house, how pretty it all was now, she started kicking something awful." Susie rubbed the side of her stomach, showing Jerry the location of the kicks.

"You think she can watch TV in there?" he asked.

"You don't know what she sees in here. She's probably learning so much watching TV with me."

Jerry side-eyed her. "Just none of those angry housewives and all that, okay?"

"Not until she's five," Susie said. She smiled, little dimples forming in her pale, freckled cheeks.

Jerry leaned over and kissed her face and then her

stomach.

"What did you eat today?" he asked.

"I was very good, thank you, doctor."

"And weight?"

"Up one more pound. I swear I'm a cow."

Jerry laughed and stretched out to go to sleep. "Just a few more weeks," he said, his voice slowing and drifting away.

"Did y'all see any elk out there?" Susie asked.

"No. Just seen where they'd been."

"Eric Deets' girl hit one today."

"In her car?" Jerry asked.

"Yeah. Your mom told me while y'all was gone. They got her over at the hospital. Saying she might not make it. It came through the window on her."

"I swear," Jerry said.

"They sure are bad this year. They ought to let y'all kill a million of them."

"I don't know. I'd be happy just to get one," said Jerry, as he slipped away to dream about doing that very thing.

CHAPTER 2

It's his daddy's people that made Andrew the way he is. There's never been nobody in our family to steal. Or use them drugs or nothing. Not until him. Even his mom, and Lord knows she has her problems. She might drink a little bit, but she never was into the drugs. She was always just after the boys who used them. And them boys could get her to do just about anything. That's been her problem, the boys.

Andrew had to get all that from his daddy's side, the stealing and the drugs. No grandchild of mine would get that from our family. No way.

I always knew Betty would have a problem being a good mother, but I prayed she'd end up with a good man and that would straighten her right out. But that didn't happen at all. She brought home that feller that would be Andrew's daddy, and I knew right off he was trouble. As soon as I laid eyes on him and I saw how Betty was looking back at him, I thought Lord have mercy, we're in for it. And we was.

It wasn't but a few months later she told me that Andrew would be coming. She told it like it was the best thing in the world that could ever happen to her, and I just went into the bathroom and balled my eyes out.

Until this one comes from Jerry's Susie - and it's supposed to be a little girl I believe - until this one comes, Andrew is the only grandchild I got. I sure wouldn't wish Andrew wasn't here, cause I always loved the little feller. But back then, I knew Betty just wasn't ready for him, and that man wasn't gonna be no help for her at all. So, I didn't want little Andrew to come. Although what I wanted sure didn't matter much.

That feller of Betty's, he put his hands on her a few times. She didn't know that I knew, but I did. We all knew, even if she didn't say nothing. Her daddy wasn't here by that time. He wouldn't have stood for that. He woulda said something to that man and told Betty not to come around the house no more if she was gonna bring him. He woulda meant it too. I just couldn't do things like that after he was gone, so I put up with that feller for them years.

Jerry put up with him too. They'd talk about the ball games and hunting and whatnot, but I could tell Jerry was not comfortable. He's always been a good, polite boy, Jerry. Even though I could tell he didn't think much of Betty's man, Jerry didn't let them know it. And he was excited to be an uncle, especially because it was going to be a little boy. Jerry always wanted me to have him a little brother, so Andrew was pretty close to that for him. And because that man of Betty's wasn't no count, Jerry has been more of a daddy to Andrew than that feller ever was.

*   *   *

11

J erry stood in aisle three of the Mountain Fishing, Hunting, Gardening and Hardware Store. Also a gas station. He checked the serial numbers and sizes on a row of small appliance seals and compared them to notes he had scribbled on a legal pad. He found the match.

Isaac, the owner of the store, smiled as Jerry approached the counter. "Jerry, what do you got today?"

"It's just a seal on Mom's garbage disposal. Been leaking pretty bad."

"Garbage disposals," Isaac said. "I've made a fortune over the years from people trying to keep them things running. Don't know that they're worth it."

"Well, Mom likes hers."

"I tell ya what, let me ring you up twice, and I'll give you the second one for half price. Just tape it to the side of the disposal, and it will be there when you have to change it again. Them things go out all the time. Might save you a trip down here."

"Sounds good. Thank ya, Isaac."

"Just grab one on your way out. How's that little lady doing, by the way?"

"Oh, she's great. Thirty-four weeks now. I got a picture here." Jerry pulled an ultrasound photo from his wallet.

"Hey Luann," Isaac yelled to his wife, as she placed price stickers on a display of Tiny Torpedo fishing lures. "Look here at Susie's baby. Jerry's got a picture."

"Hey Jerry," Luann said. She reached out and patted his shoulder as she passed him.

Jerry smiled and nodded to her. "Luann."

"Oh, let me see that little thing," Luann said, excitement in her voice. "I didn't think she was due for a while yet. I just talked to your mom the other day, and she said--"

"It's not a real baby picture," Isaac interrupted. He handed the ultrasound photo to her. "It's one of them still-in-the-stomach pictures."

"Let me see that anyway," Luann said. She studied the picture before holding it up beside Jerry's face. He grinned uncomfortably as she said, "I know'd I'd seen that chin somewhere before."

"Let's hope she gets the rest of her looks from her mother," Isaac added.

After more small talk with Isaac and Luann, Jerry completed the purchase, retrieved the extra seal and left the store. On the way to his patrol car, he looked up the road and saw a blue Acura fishtail through a mountain turn and accelerate into a straight stretch as it approached the store. It was moving. The thundering engine went quiet, just as the tires screamed and rubber smoke filled the air. The driver had seen Jerry's patrol car and stomped his brake pedal. His skidding path burned on the road in parallel, twisting lines. As he passed the parking lot, he looked toward the store and locked eyes with the uniformed deputy.

Jerry raced to his patrol car, tossed the garbage disposal seals in the passenger's seat, ignited his engine and tore out of the parking lot, forming a cloud of dirt and gravel behind him. Jerry checked his mirror and saw some of the debris hitting the store.

"Damn, sorry Isaac."

He caught the car a few miles later and pulled over seventeen-year-old Bradley Donaldson in the Acura. Jerry noticed the license plate was for the neighboring county. After he radioed in the information, he approached the car. "You seem to be in an awful big hurry, buddy."

"I guess," Bradley said, giving him a benign, absent glare.

Jerry retrieved the boy's driver's license and registration. "A Donaldson? And from Letcher County?" Jerry asked. "Car like this must mean you're some of Dr. Donaldson's people?"

"That's my daddy," said Bradley.

"You're a long way from home, Mr. Donaldson," said Jerry.

"I'm coming to see my girlfriend."

"And who might that be?"

"Jess Reynolds. Taking her to the fireworks tonight."

Jerry thought about that. "Fred and Kathy Reynolds' daughter?"

"Yeah, I believe that's her mom and dad."

"She's certainly a nice girl," said Jerry, "but not worth getting a speeding ticket over. I'm gonna have to write you up. Sixty-three in a forty-five. And that's after you saw me. I probably should throw in reckless driving, but I guess you did a good job keeping her on the road. I'll give you that, at least."

"You could just let me go," suggested Bradley. "You know, with a warning."

"Oh yeah? And why would I do that?"

"Cause it's just a waste of time," said Bradley. "You know who my daddy is. He will--"

"This aint about your father," Jerry interrupted. "This is about you. You're breaking the law. These roads are dangerous. Young girl is in the hospital right now because she ran into an elk yesterday. Probably wasn't speeding nothing like you were neither."

"I aint gonna hit no elk."

"And some of these guardrails aint the best in our

14

county, I hate to say. Hit some of them just right, and you'll rocket right over into Troublesome Creek. They might not find you for days."

Bradley watched as Jerry continued to write.

"You know, like I said, Daddy will just get this taken care of. I won't be in no trouble." Bradley remained calm, unemotional and practical. He knew the score, and Jerry did too, even if he pretended otherwise.

"That'd sure make things a lot easier for me when your daddy's people call my boss and yell at him," said Jerry.

"So, I can go?"

"No." Jerry finished the ticket. "Sign this here. Not an admission of guilt, just a promise you'll appear in court."

"I'll sign it. But I won't be there," said Bradley. "Daddy will--"

"Take care of it," continued Jerry. "You've said that three times now. Just curious how do you think he'll feel when his insurance goes up a couple hundred dollars a month on account of you?"

"You'll have to ask him." Bradley smiled as he took the ticket. "Can I go now?"

Jerry nodded. He watched Bradley start his car and pull away. When he darted onto the road, Bradley fired the engine and accelerated into a curve, gaining speed as he rounded a mountain bend and disappeared from Jerry's view.

*   *   *

Jerry and Susie arrived at the parking lot of their local high school. The Buckner County High School football team played their home games on a field that rested on

15

a little hill behind and above the school. Attendees to games parked in the school lot and walked a hundred yards, mainly uphill, to the bleacher seats.

Jerry activated his hazard lights and began driving up the service road to the field.

"Where are you going?" Susie asked.

"I'm going to drop you off up there and come back here and park."

"You are not dropping me off up there, leaving me like I'm some kind of helpless fool who can't walk up a hill."

"But--"

"I can walk up there just fine," Susie interrupted. "I'm pregnant. I aint disabled."

"The doctor said you shouldn't exert yourself."

"I will not get out up there, Jerry Somerset. No way. I won't stand there by myself and see everybody point at how big I am. Lord have mercy. You turn around and park down here. I'm walking with you."

On the Fourth of July, the football field doubled as the venue for the county fireworks display put on by the local chapter of the U.S. Jaycees. Jerry and Susie were early, with the show a few hours away. They could mingle with the people of the county. Eat a hot dog maybe.

Jerry located the closest parking space at the bottom of the hill. "Is this far enough away or should we park across the street at the car wash?"

"This is fine," Susie said, checking her face in the mirror. She smiled at herself and saw a speck of lipstick in her mouth, a merlot star centered on one of her large upper teeth. "Oh Jesus," she said, brushing it away with her index finger. "Would you have let me walk around looking like that?"

They exited the vehicle and began the walk to the field. "Hey Jerry, hey Susie," people said as they walked ahead of them, the couple slowing and giving ground for others to pass.

"Jerry, you should have driven that momma-to-be up there and dropped her off," one man said.

"I know," Jerry answered. "Where are my manners?"

The chain-link fence along the road to the field was lined with advertisements for local businesses: Isaac's store, The Buckner County Times, Piggly Wiggly. Other signs were paid for by politicians running in the fall election. There were magistrates, the county judge executive, who was running unopposed, and a half dozen people trying to become jailer.

Halfway up the hill, Susie paused to catch her breath. She leaned on a light pole. "Let's rest here just for a minute."

Above Susie on the pole was a campaign poster that read, "Little Dan Calhoun for State Congress" with a large photo of Big Dan's twenty-nine-year-old son smiling back at the world. Square jaw, big straight teeth, a little gel in his hair. Dressed in his uniform as the county sheriff, the handsome fellow in this picture could sell a record player to a deaf man.

Susie looked up and rolled her eyes. "These signs are everywhere. Everyone knows he's gonna win. They're just wasting money on all these things."

Nate Hoskins, a recent retiree from the gas company, approached Jerry and Susie on his way up the hill. He pointed to the sign and asked Jerry, "You about to lose your boss to Frankfurt?"

"Maybe," said Jerry. "As long as folks like you get out and vote for him. He needs everybody's support. Big election."

"Oh, I'm voting for him for sure," Nate said proudly. "Told Big Dan my whole family's voting for Danny just last week."

Nate turned his attention from the poster back to Jerry. "But once he wins, who'll be sheriff in his place?"

"I'm not sure how that'll work," Jerry responded, pretending not to know the answer. "I think there will be one of those, what do they call it, a special election."

"Ought to be you," Nate said. "Lord knows we need a good feller for the job, with all the craziness around here these days."

"Um-hmm," Susie agreed. "Shoulda been him last time."

Jerry snapped a look in her direction. He raised his eyebrows slightly, convincing her not to continue the subject.

*   *   *

Jerry and Susie sat on the first row of the full bleachers, facing the field. The Combs Brothers, a bluegrass band, picked out and twanged songs like *Mountain Dew* and heard approving calls from old-timers as they sang about jugs of homemade liquor. The brothers were dressed in burgundy suits, with bright red Kentucky Colonel ties. Between songs, they teased the crowd with promises that the fireworks were just a few minutes away. Always, just a few minutes away.

Nearly everyone who passed Jerry and Susie on their way to the higher seats waved or smiled or spoke to the couple. Susie lost track of the times she said, "Just a few more weeks," to ladies who pressed her on her big day. They both had a hot dog, the good grilled ones with burned black stripes in the skin. Jerry took his with a packet of mustard. Susie, the works. She even sent Jerry back to the concession stand for another one, along with a bag of popcorn for them to split.

Most people in Buckner County would not consider bluegrass music to be among their chosen forms of entertainment, but that fact would not be realized by measuring the appreciation of the Fourth of July crowd. The Combs Brothers were gifted showmen, and they reminded many in the audience of their long-dead grandparents who always had banjo and fiddle music playing in their cars or on console radios in their living rooms. For one day a year, people who had traded those songs for rock or country or hip-hop music allowed themselves to marinate in the sounds of their youth and were excited to sing along to the tale of Dooley, the good old man who lived below the mill.

"Dooley, give me a swaller and I'll pay you back someday," the crowd roared in unison.

The Combs Brothers continued to play as the sun tried to find a mountain behind which to disappear for the night. Eventually, Charles, the older of the two brothers, unbuckled his banjo strap and approached the microphone. "Alright boys, hit them lights," he said, just before the breaker switches popped and the field lights went dark.

The crowd whooped in appreciation.

Two rockets thumped out of their metal tubes and sizzled into the air. The first broke into a hundred tiny sparkles, just before the second boomed and exploded into a collection of cascading reds and blues.

*   *   *

Stanley Jennings helped with the fireworks for years.

Although an active member of the Jaycees in his youth and a lifelong supporter, this year Stanley missed the event. He was home in bed, recovering from knee surgery. His forty-two-year-old daughter, Alison, and her son visited him earlier on their way to the fireworks.

"Daddy, if you let me turn your bed toward the window, I bet you'd see everything."

"Oh, that's all right. I'm gonna take me one of them pills yonder when you leave. I'll have my own fireworks show here real soon."

The doctors sent Stanley home with a large bottle of generic ten-milligram oxycodone, and Stanley counted the minutes until the next dose.

By the time that blue and red fireball exploded in the sky to the south of his house, Stanley was wrapped in the warm embrace of an opioid slumber. No knee pain, no worries, no regrets. Just deep, fulfilling rest. He dreamed about the wife he lost a decade earlier to lung cancer. He dreamed about the five years he coached Little League baseball so his grandsons could play for him. He dreamed about his days as a young man, hunting and fishing Troublesome Creek, the waterway where he learned mountain lessons about friendship, loyalty and justice.

With the oxycodone guiding his dreams and fueling his imagination, all the memories from his past were sculpted and shaded into scenes from a better life, a happier life.

His sleep was so absolute, he did not notice the two young men standing at the foot of his bed. Both were dressed in jeans and black hoodies. They wore gloves and Halloween masks. One was a devil, with a black and red striped face, yellow teeth and horns. The other mask was pale white, with a goofy smile, exposed pink tongue, and blue half-moons under his eyes. Had Stanley lived a hundred years, he could not have predicted that one of the faces of the two men who would kill him would be obstructed by a Halloween mask of Casper, the Friendly Ghost.

*　　　　　*　　　　　*

Susie squeezed Jerry's thigh and leaned her head on his shoulder. A dozen small rockets exploded together, lighting up the darkness with white and yellow streaks. Jerry glanced over and saw Susie's eyes looking back at him. She reached her hand and caught his chin, holding it long enough to kiss him. The two shared a long embrace, as the field was bathed in fading, glowing embers. The remains landed in the grass and fizzled before dying.

*　　　　　*　　　　　*

Casper noticed the table beside Stanley's bed was covered with get-well-soon cards. He picked up one and looked at it. On it was a convalescent dog, wearing a cone around its neck. The card read, "At least you won't have to wear one of these…until you start licking yourself."

In the middle of the table was a floral arrangement. Yellow daisies and red carnations placed inside a mug branded for chicken noodle soup. Casper sniffed the flowers to test their authenticity.

Devil walked to the side of the bed and smacked Stanley on the shoulder. "Wake up, old man."

"Woe, woe. No need to hurt him," Casper said, elbowing Devil out of the way and taking his place beside Stanley.

Stanley's head snapped off the pillow. His eyes blinked, as he tried to make sense of the situation.

"Hey sir," Casper said. "It's okay. We're not gonna hurt ya or nothing. Just get up for a minute."

Stanley tried to surge forward, but Casper held him in place. Gentle, but firm.

"Just relax," said Casper.

Outside, an explosion caught Stanley's attention, and he looked out his window to see the skies lit up with streaking balls of blues and greens and reds. His daughter was right; he did have a nice view.

"We're not here to hurt ya," repeated Casper. "We just want some stuff and we'll be gone."

"I aint got nothing," said Stanley. "You just get on out of here."

Devil tossed aside some of the cards and retrieved a medicine bottle on the table. "Aint got nothing? Well, I see something right here." He pocketed the oxycodone.

"Okay," said Stanley. "Is that what you want? That's fine. I just had knee surgery. Them's some good pills, all right. And there's some more through yonder in the bathroom. They was giving them to me before the surgery. They aint as strong, but they're okay. You take them too."

"Oh, we will," said Devil.

"And then y'all leave," demanded Stanley.

Devil stepped into the bathroom. On the sink, he saw a ceramic jar labeled "Chopper Hopper." Beside it, another prescription bottle. Devil looked at the label and called to Stanley. "You talking about these Percocets?"

"Yeah, you find them?" Stanley called back.

"I found them. Is that all you got in here?" Devil

Troublesome Creek

shoveled toothpaste and mouthwash out of the medicine cabinet. A bottle of antacids fell to the floor and popped open, scattering tablets across the tiles and behind the toilet.

"That's it unless you want my hemorrhoid cream too."

Devil returned to the bedroom and saw a little smirk on the old man's face. Casper leaned toward the hallway. He said, "You get them? Let's go then."

"Hold on a minute," said Devil, motioning for Casper to return his attention to guarding Stanley. Devil approached a gun cabinet in the corner. Through the glass doors, he saw a rifle and a shotgun. He tried opening the door, but it was locked. He picked up the chicken soup bowl and aimed it at the glass doors.

"Wait!" Casper said. He looked to Stanley. "Is there a key?"

"On top there, behind a little ledge," Stanley answered.

Devil reached on top of the gun case, retrieved the key and opened the doors. Inside was a 12-gauge Remington shotgun, the 870 Wingmaster model popular for squirrel hunting. Also snug inside its velvet fetter was a .30-06 Springfield bolt action rifle. Had Stanley ever been selected in the annual elk hunt lottery, this gun would have accompanied him into the woods to bag his trophy.

Devil cradled the two guns and nodded to his partner.

"Is that enough?" asked Casper.

"Yeah, let's go."

Casper returned to Stanley and said, "Now, we're gonna leave, but don't do nothing stupid. Just roll over and count to a hundred."

"Two hundred," insisted Devil.

"After that, you can call the cops or whatever," said Casper. "But we wasn't mean to you, so you ought not be telling them nothing about us, okay?"

Stanley nodded.

"So, roll over," Casper repeated.

Stanley did as instructed, but he then slid his left hand under the pillow on the other side of the bed. He gripped the cold black handle of the snub-nose Smith & Wesson thirty-eight that had been his only nocturnal companion for the last ten years.

"Watch him!" yelled Devil. "That's a gun!"

Stanley rolled over and fired a shot at Casper. He missed. Casper jumped on the bed, catapulting the gun out of Stanley's hand and onto the floor. Stanley grabbed Casper around the neck. With the intruder in a headlock, the old man stuck his thumb through the eyehole of the Casper mask. He pushed until he felt the eyeball move and tried to get his thumbnail behind it.

Casper screamed and wrestled himself away from the old man. With his good leg, Stanley front-kicked Casper in the chest, sending him off the side of the bed and crashing into the wall. A long crack formed in the drywall from the impact.

Devil put down the rifle and shotgun and jumped on the bed. As he attacked Stanley, the old man tried to push him away by putting the palm of his hand on Devil's throat and pushing hard. Stanley's hand slipped under the mask and popped the rubber disguise into the air. It landed on the bottom of the bed.

Devil tried covering his face, but Stanley saw his full, lumberjack beard, well-manicured and as red as a firetruck. Devil put the mask back on just as he saw Stanley throw himself into the floor, hungry for his gun.

Devil pounced on it at the same time, and the two men struggled for control.

The gun fired, and Stanley screamed.

Devil stood, holding the gun. He stepped back slowly from the old man.

"You shot him," screamed Casper, getting to his feet and trying to regain his vision. "You shot him!"

"No, I didn't shoot him. It just went off, the gun."

"Ohmygod, ohmygod, ohmygod," repeated Casper.

"You bastards," Stanley said, trying to stand to take one more swing at the two men. But he collapsed back into the floor. He was gut shot. The 145-grain lead round had passed through the surface of the right lobe of his liver and exploded out of the back of the organ, leaving a symmetrical star-shaped exit wound the coroner said reminded him of the top of a Christmas tree.

"I'm so sorry," Casper said. "We, we, we didn't--"

Devil cut him off. "Let's go! We gotta get out of here."

Casper looked back at Stanley and saw the man holding his bloody hands in front of him.

"I'm sorry, Coach," said Casper. "I swear. We didn't mean it. We weren't gonna hurt you. We weren't. I swear."

"We aint got time for this," said Devil.

"Let's call 9-1-1," said Casper. "We just can't leave him like this."

"They record those calls. They'll figure it out. Come on."

Devil put his hand on Casper's back and ushered him out of the room. They walked through the kitchen and arrived at the door to the outside.

Devil stopped. "Wait," he said.

"What?"

Devil looked back toward the bedroom. "He saw me."

"He saw you?"

"Yeah. My mask was off for a second, and he saw me. Probably."

"Probably?"

"I had my hands up and covered my face, but yeah, he probably saw me."

Casper looked back to the room. He saw Stanley struggling to get to his feet. "Do you even know him?" he asked Devil. "Would he know you, like recognize you?"

"He could describe me," Devil said. He switched to a whisper and continued, "And yeah, everybody knows me. He would too. You know who my daddy is. Everybody knows us."

"So what? What are you gonna do about it? There's nothing we can do."

"We gotta go back and finish it," Devil answered.

"Finish it?"

"Yeah, finish it." Devil held up the Smith & Wesson.

"No. No way."

"He didn't see you, so you wouldn't understand."

"No. We aint doing this."

"Fine. I'll do it myself," Devil said, as he took steps toward the bedroom.

"Wait," Casper yelled at him. "Your keys are in the truck. If you go in that room, when you come out, I'll be gone."

"No, you won't. You won't leave me here."

"I will. I swear to God I will. We aint gonna kill nobody. That in there was just an accident. But this would be on purpose. No way. That's wrong, killing something on purpose."

Devil continued toward the bedroom.

"I'm leaving," Casper said, starting to open the screen door. "I mean it."

Devil stopped. He looked back at Casper and nodded in defeat. "Fine, let's go. He probably won't make it anyway."

The two ran out of the house. Devil tossed the gun in the backyard. The boys cut through the garden Stanley had not maintained in weeks. The limbs of his tomato plants had fallen to the ground and were being overtaken by weeds and grass. A green pepper, the first of the year, was starting to wither and wrinkle. It should have been picked a week ago.

The boys disappeared into the woods above the garden. They ran up the hill behind the house, adrenalin fueling them up the terrain like mountain goats. Once they crossed that hill, they saw Sawmill Holler on the other side. Troublesome Creek provided the last obstacle before reaching their truck. They hid it in that holler so nobody saw it near Stanley's house. After they waded across the Troublesome, they would be free to drive away with their loot.

Back inside the house, Stanley saw the fireworks continue to light up the night sky. He struggled to pull himself onto the bed, but he collapsed back onto his walnut hardwood floor. His legs stopped working. With his forearms and elbows, he propelled himself toward the hallway, a few inches at a time. He grabbed the doorframe and pulled himself into a sitting position. Each breath was shorter than the one before. Covered in death sweat, Stanley looked at the wall phone in the kitchen, twenty feet away.

* * *

The last glowing cinder faded in the grass of the football field. Circuit boxes popped, and the field lights illuminated. The citizens of Buckner County began gathering their blankets and coolers. Over the public-address system, a voice thanked everyone for attending and announced a collection of the Combs Brothers greatest hits would play until everyone was gone.

"But you don't have to run off," the announcer said. "Hang around for a few minutes. You might run into somebody you aint seen for a while. And you can say hello."

After the announcement, the Combs Brothers' rendition of *Fox on the Run* filled the air. Jerry and Susie stayed seated, as the crowd filed passed them. They waved again to the same folks they had greeted earlier in the evening.

"You get that little lady home, Jerry. Needs her feet up," someone said.

* * *

Stanley's cell phone was closer than the wall-mounted device in the kitchen. It was charging on the six-drawer oak dresser on the other side of his bed. He knew, however, that he would have to be under the window on the other side of the room to get a signal. And that was not even a guarantee. During the summer, the full poplar trees on the hill behind his house disrupted his cell service, with July being the worst time to make a call all year. He decided to drag himself to the reliable kitchen phone, as he did not want his dying thoughts to be about the failures of modern technology.

The phone in the kitchen presented its own problem, as it required him to stand to make the call. It was the same wall-mounted rotary phone that his parents had acquired in the 1960s, when they lived in this house and Stanley was a teenager. The size of a shoebox and with innards crafted out of heavy metals, the bright orange behemoth weighed as much as a newborn baby and was consistently the first item mentioned when Stanley had a visitor.

"Is that thing real?" they asked. "Does it still work?"

It did, but Stanley did not get many calls on it. His friends and family members knew to text him on his cell phone, and he called them back from one of his three "good spots" for cell service. Usually the front porch. When the orange phone rang, it was a telemarketer or someone from long ago. Unlike modern phones and their canned ringtones that mimic banging metal, the rotary phone actually rang. A small hammer vibrated between two brass hemispheres inside and sang its announcement. Stanley liked that he heard misses and flaws in the clangs. Modern phones played the same tune each time, but when his orange phone called to him, it was always slightly different than the time before and full of perfect imperfections.

Stanley had to cross what looked to be a continent of linoleum to use it now. The pain from his abdomen felt hot and wet, and it was not exclusive to the wound. The ball of ache splintered in every direction and shot barbs and brambles throughout his body. Turn the wrong way and a bolt of electricity passed through his groin and ran down his leg. When he felt the pain was the worst thing imaginable, he was overtaken by the need to cough and then experienced a new level of torture.

Stanley was dying. He knew he was dying. At a quarter of the distance he needed to drag himself, he accepted it. He stopped under a picture hanging in his kitchen of a creek baptism. His mother's favorite painting, by local artist Paul Brett Johnson, showed an old preacher dressed in a white shirt and suspenders, with his congregation spread across the creekbank. Some members looked down in the water from a small wooden bridge as they watched the preacher bathe the newest member of his flock in the word of God. The baptized was an old woman, draped in a white robe, with a white garment wrapped around her head. Serene, emotionless. She too looked at the end of her life, and she sought to extend it in these waters.

Under the painting, Stanley lost any remaining control of his body. The blurry room spun. His left hand was in a fist, pushing on the floor and anchoring his weight, keeping his head from pitching forward. He steadied himself by placing his right hand on the cream-colored kitchen wall. When he pulled it back, he saw a bloody handprint remain. A crimson outline of his five fingers and palm. He realized this handprint could be the last evidence that Stanley Jennings ever existed. His last action, his last moment. Every choice he made in life, every place he visited, every person he knew, it all ended with meaningless blood on a wall.

His last decision though was to change that, to have his final action matter. He rubbed his hand on his damp stomach and placed his freshly bloodied index finger on the wall. He steadied his hand and wrote a large red C on the painted surface.

*　　　　　*　　　　　*

Susie looked over the crowd and waived to her mother-in-law. "There's your mom," she said to Jerry.

Mary, sixty-one-years-old, was in a crowd of other older women, all smiling and making promises to see each other more often. Jerry and Susie approached.

"It calls for one whole cup of sugar, but I only use two tablespoons," Mary explained to the group. "I never liked my pickles to be too sweet."

"Me neither," one of them replied.

"I like mine sweet," another lady countered.

"Well, you can use the full cup then," said Mary. "I'll add a tad more as the season goes on and them cucumbers get a little bitter. I might go up to three or four tablespoons. But not a whole cup. You don't need a whole cup of sugar in your pickles."

Jerry put his arm on his mother's shoulders, resting it on the same red, white and blue windbreaker she wore every year to the fireworks.

"Y'all better get her recipe," he said. "She won't have any jars to spare."

"Jerry sure likes his pickles," Mary said. "Andrew too."

"They're awful valuable around the house," Jerry continued. "She'll even hide them when company comes over."

"I do not, Jerry. That's a lie. Y'all don't believe a word he says."

The women laughed.

"Mary, we'll see you at that fruit tree grafting class next week, okay?" one of the women said, as she took steps toward the hill, leading down to the parking lot.

"I'll see you girls there," she answered. "I've always wanted me some fruit trees."

Mary's friends left her alone with Jerry and Susie.

"You don't need anything more to can, Mom," said Jerry.

"Oh shush, Jerry," Susie said, defending her mother-in-law. "You won't be complaining when she's got some canned peaches for a fresh cobbler in February."

Jerry looked around. "Did Andrew come with you? I aint seen him here."

Mary shook her head no.

"We thought he was coming with you," Susie said.

"Aint seen him or Betty all day," said Mary. "It's untelling where that boy's at."

*　　　　　*　　　　　*

Casper and Devil waded through Troublesome Creek. Devil held the guns over his head, making sure not to get them wet. On the other side of the creek, the boys ran up a bank to the awaiting green Ford pickup truck. Devil retrieved the keys hidden under the driver's seat and started it. Casper jumped into the passenger's seat, as Devil removed his mask.

"Take that thing off," Devil said. "Somebody's gonna see you like that."

*　　　　　*　　　　　*

Jerry felt a smack on his back and heard, "Jerry, when you gonna let this little gal have her baby?" He turned to see Big Dan standing behind him.

"I don't know. She sure aint waiting for my permission. I've been ready for a while now."

"I aint ready just yet though," said Susie. "And I'm the one that counts."

Big Dan laughed. "That was some show tonight,

32

wasn't it?"

"Always," said Mary. "Every year is better than the last one."

"The girls up at the restaurant are staying open late tonight for the fireworks crowd," said Big Dan. "Y'all should stop and have a slice of pie."

"Oh, that'll be fun," said Mary. "If Susie's up for it."

"That does sound good," said Susie. "You know, one time up there I had a slice of a pie I'd never had before."

"And what was that?" Big Dan asked.

"I believe y'all called it applesauce something. Custard maybe? An applesauce custard pie?"

"Yeah, that's what it's called. That was a recipe from my Great Aunt Evelyn in Arkansas. Mom would make that for us when we was kids, and boy did I love it. When we opened the restaurant, I made sure one of the gals could make it."

"Reckon they'll have one tonight?" asked Susie.

"Let's see." Big Dan pulled out his cellphone and dialed. He reached one of the workers at his restaurant. After discussing the size of the crowd and letting her know the fireworks event had let out, Big Dan gave her one last directive. "Y'all make sure you get one of them applesauce custards in the oven, okay? Got some VIPs heading that way, wanting a bite of one."

Susie looked to Jerry and grinned.

*   *   *

Jerry maneuvered through the congested parking lot, nodding and waving to people who allowed his entry into the row of cars.

"Reckon where Andrew is?" Susie asked.

"No idea," said Jerry. "He could be getting into anything these days."

At the exit of the parking lot, Jerry pulled to the side and motioned for cars to go around him.

"Mom's car is way back there. I'll wait and let her follow us. She don't like to drive at night."

Mary's sedan snaked through the rows and medians and arrived at the exit. She flipped her lights at Jerry, and he pulled out of the lot ahead of her. They drove west on Route 550 toward Calhoun's Restaurant, five miles away.

On the two-lane road, Jerry approached a bend just as a green Ford pickup truck came out of the curve going in the opposite direction. The truck darted out of the turn at a high rate of speed and crossed the double yellow line with its front left wheel. Jerry swerved to avoid a collision. He glanced over and saw the driver of the truck. He knew the young man immediately from his manicured lumberjack beard, red as a firetruck. Jerry saw another person was in the passenger's seat, but he did not get a clear look at him.

"Good lord," said Susie. "There goes a lunatic."

Jerry looked in his rearview mirror and saw Mary's car swerve as well. She ran off the road onto the shoulder. Jerry slowed and watched Mary pull back onto the road and continue to follow him.

"Is your mom okay?" Susie asked.

"Looks like she is," he answered.

"Lord have mercy. People's crazy," Susie declared.

Jerry again looked behind his car and caught the last glimpse of the pickup truck, barreling into the next curve and disappearing into the darkness.

"Aren't you going to do something?" asked Susie.

"Do something? Like what?"

"I don't know. Go get him."

"One, not with you in the car. And two, don't you know whose truck that was?"

"No."

"That's Steven Calhoun." said Jerry.

"So."

"So, unless he just killed somebody, I aint touching that."

"You at least need to call Danny and tell him."

"Tell him what?" Jerry asked.

"That his brother's out hot-rodding like that."

"Hot-rodding?" Jerry said. "Did you just say hot-rodding?"

Susie did not acknowledge the question.

$$*\qquad\qquad*\qquad\qquad*$$

"If Big Dan comes in here, I'm telling him about seeing his boy out there driving like that," said Mary, as she sat with Jerry and Susie at a table in Calhoun's Restaurant. A dozen other tables were filled, mostly with people having desserts. One group of teenagers scarfed down hamburgers and onion rings in a corner booth.

"Just leave it alone, Mom," said Jerry.

"Could've run both of us off the road," she replied, raising her voice. "And Susie the way she is. You think about that?"

"Yeah, but that's also why we need to stop talking about this," Jerry said, trying to emphasize the calm in his voice. "We need to talk about something else. Something less stressful."

"That's right," Mary said, remembering that Susie had been told to avoid stress. "It's just that somebody ought to--"

35

"Mom," Jerry cut her off.

"Okay, okay," she answered. With a light touch, Mary rubbed her hand over the linen tablecloth in front of her, trying to push a small wrinkle off the table. "This thing is brand new. Feel it."

Jerry and Susie patted the tablecloth.

"It is nice," confirmed Susie.

The worst kept secret in Buckner County was that Calhoun's Restaurant never turned a profit. With low prices and high wages to attract the best workers, Big Dan allowed it to lose money, month after month. He would not sacrifice the kind of quality he wanted in his restaurant simply because he lived in a sparsely populated county that could not provide the necessary revenue. So Big Dan provided it himself. Calhoun's featured mahogany walls, dark cherry upholstered chairs, polished silverware and the only dining room in three counties where the workers would never be seen wearing jeans.

Big Dan did not skimp on food either. He had arrangements with local farmers for in-season garden vegetables, fresh eggs and orchard fruits. But in Eastern Kentucky, no meal is complete without an ample serving of meat. Big Dan paid one farmer to raise and slaughter one thousand jumbo Cornish Rock chickens for him every year. Any steaks served at Calhoun's came from eleven-month-old red Angus steers raised on the open pastures of a farm in Montgomery County. A piece of meat that would cost fifty dollars at a steakhouse in Lexington or Louisville could be had Friday nights at Calhoun's for $9.99, and people packed the little restaurant those nights to carve them up.

The server arrived with three large slices of applesauce custard pie. Jerry caught a whiff of the brown sugar, cinnamon and vanilla medley as the server passed them out.

"Boy, that sure smells good," he said.

"Wait till you try it," the server said. "This is my favorite."

Behind the server, another worker carried a tub of vanilla ice cream, still wafting frozen vapor like a locomotive leaving a steam trail. "Big Dan likes us to add the ice cream at the table, so it don't melt too fast," the first server said. "Who wants some?"

They all three asked for their slice to be topped. The server covered the still bubbling applesauce filler with small round scoops of ice cream that squirmed and danced atop the pie. The server nodded approval to her three hungry guests, and they each plucked their first bites with oversized spoons.

"My word," said Mary.

The server smiled in satisfaction and left the table. She and the other workers began stripping the empty tables of their tablecloths and place settings. On Wednesday nights, all employees of Calhoun's stayed late to prepare the restaurant for the Thursday morning crowd. They would wash the linens, dust the lightbulbs, steam the water glasses and clean the windows. Everything had to be spotless and in order before they opened on Thursday morning, but not because they expected an early crowd. Everyone in town knew not to walk in the door at Calhoun's until after ten o'clock on Thursday mornings, unless they were invited to be there by Big Dan personally. Everyone stayed away and did not enjoy the buffet of sausage gravy and biscuits, buttermilk pancakes, and three kinds of breakfast pork. Big Dan's best cook, Ellen Jacobs, was always there on Thursday mornings to fix eggs every way eggs can be made. She would prepare them fresh, cracking the shells as she saw invitees enter the restaurant.

"Two over easy, Mayor?" she would say as Mayor Benny Baker passed the counter on the way to the dining area.

"You know it, Ellen," he would return. "Nobody makes my eggs like you do."

The mayor was there every Thursday morning. The county judge executive too. Big Dan was always there, and anyone else Big Dan decided needed to be there. Sometimes Eddie from The Buckner County Times attended if Big Dan needed something said in the newspaper. Politicians and business owners from neighboring counties would be there if they had business with the men in the room. After Little Dan became sheriff, Big Dan allowed him to attend Thursday breakfast twice a month. He was not welcome every week, however, because sometimes things had to be discussed that the sheriff would not need to hear.

Every Thursday, decisions were made about what enterprises would be allowed in Buckner County, what contractors would get jobs for county roads or bridges, who would win upcoming elections, and what offers would be accepted for homes in important neighborhoods. But the budget, that's where they spent most of their time. State programs, federal programs, coal severance settlements, money for the arts: any penny that flowed on the river of dollars coming into Buckner County got diverted and dispersed in Big Dan's restaurant on Thursday mornings, while three men sopped biscuits and stacked pancakes.

Once the meetings began at eight o'clock, the restaurant staff knew to stay in the backroom for the first hour. They gave the guests sixty undisturbed minutes before coming out to freshen the table and help the men finish their work before ten. A few times, the men would run late, and the staff would have to stand at the front door and ask people to come back later.

One Thursday four years earlier, the men stayed until almost noon, as they dealt with the sudden departure of Sheriff Bolling and debated who would replace him. The Kentucky Constitution says that decision is made by the county judge executive, but that was a duty the sitting judge, Alex Wicker, knew he needed to bring to Calhoun's for discussion.

For most of that morning, if Jerry could have heard the conversation around the breakfast table, he would have prepared to accept a promotion to sheriff. All the men agreed Jerry was perfect for the job: good family man, churchgoer, always a splendid demeanor. He never made mistakes and did not have an enemy in the entire county.

"If any of my girls had ended up with a boy from Buckner County," Judge Wicker said. "I would have wanted it to be a feller like Jerry."

"Yessir," agreed Mayor Baker.

The other man to be considered for sheriff that morning was Big Dan's son Danny. Although without a law enforcement background, Big Dan said his son was raised to lead. He grew up around important men and knew how things were supposed to work. He could learn on the job and take direction from the mayor and the judge.

The mayor pointed out Little Dan's youth.

"All the Kentucky Constitution says is a sheriff needs to be twenty-four years old and live in the county," Big Dan said. "He'll work with you boys. He will. I know he will."

When they finally put it to ballot, Jerry had two votes to be sheriff and Little Dan had one. But Little Dan had the one vote that mattered.

Jerry watched Mary take her last bite from the pie and said, "I'd say they're about ready for all of us to clear out of here."

"Oh, y'all are fine," the server said, as she wiped down a table in the corner.

"Naw, we better head on out or else you might hand me a mop," Jerry said and reached to help Susie out of her seat.

"We could sure use you," the server said before turning her attention to Susie. "You look so good, Susie. You've got the best color to your cheeks, I swear."

"Thank you, but I don't feel it," Susie said, "I aint getting out again unless I have to. The next time you see me, I'll look a whole lot better with this thing out of me."

"Bless your heart," the server said. "Can we get you anything before you leave?"

"Reckon y'all have a couple more pieces of that pie?" Mary asked. She looked to Jerry and said, "I'd like to take some to Betty and Andrew."

"Best I remember there was still a chunk of it left," the server said. "Want me to cut it in half for them?"

*   *   *

Jerry's cruiser rolled up the gravel driveway, followed by Mary's sedan. Jerry's trailer sat a hundred feet away from his mother's house in what used to be part of her yard. Someone sitting on Jerry's front porch could have a conversation with another person on Mary's without having to raise their voices. Such conversations happened often.

Jerry parked in one of the two gravel spaces in front of his trailer, and Mary pulled her car next to her front porch. Lights were on in the backyard behind Mary's house. From the cruiser, Jerry and Susie saw Andrew behind the house with a rake in his hand.

"Well, there he is," said Susie. "What in the world is he doing back there this late?"

"I'll go see," said Jerry.

Jerry got out of his car and went around to help Susie out on her side. He walked her to the porch of their trailer and opened the door. After turning on the lights and looking around, he began to walk back outside. "I'll make sure mom gets in and then go check on him."

"I'm going straight to bed," Susie said. She reached her arms out to him, and Jerry stepped back in the kitchen to hug and kiss her.

After their embrace, Jerry stepped out of his house and off his front porch. He saw Mary walking up the steps to her house, carrying her purse and two Styrofoam boxes. Mary looked to Jerry.

"What's he doing back there?" she asked.

"Probably working on that turkey run," Jerry answered.

"This late?"

Jerry shrugged.

Mary entered her house and saw her thirty-eight-year-old daughter, Betty, asleep in front of the television in the living room. Jerry followed her inside. Mary turned to Jerry and put her finger to her lips as a request for him to be quiet around his sleeping sister.

Jerry shook his head no and turned on the lights in the hallway and kitchen. He walked loudly over the creaking floorboards.

"I'm trying to sleep here," Betty mumbled, extending her hand to block the light from the kitchen.

"Don't you have a bedroom?" Jerry asked. "Mom don't need to tiptoe around her house because you can't find your room."

"It's fine, Jerry," Mary said.

"I was just watching tv, and I guess I fell asleep," Betty said. She sat up on the couch, wrapping the blanket around her shoulders and straightening her mangled t-shirt to cover her stomach. Still dressed in the clothes she wore earlier in the day, her jean shorts were unbuttoned and had slid down her legs.

"Where have you been all day?" asked Mary.

"I was at the lake with a handsome stranger," Betty said, trying to slip the shorts over her hips without being noticed. "We lounged on his yacht and went for a private helicopter ride."

"Oh Jesus," said Jerry.

"And was Andrew with you?" Mary asked.

"She wasn't at the lake on a yacht, Mom," Jerry said.

"I can't keep up with him," Betty said, as she buttoned her shorts.

"You're his mother," said Mary. "You're supposed to keep up with him."

"He's twenty-one years old, Mom," Betty answered.

"You kept a good eye on him his first twenty years?" Jerry asked. "Is that what you're saying? You need a break from all those mother-of-the-year awards?"

"Jerry!" Mary snapped.

Betty sprung from the couch and stomped toward the hallway, dragging her blanket with her.

"I brought you some pie from Calhoun's," Mary said to her daughter.

"Don't want it," Betty barked. She stopped and looked back at her brother. "When you have one, Jerry, you'll see it aint so easy. You think you're all high and mighty, but I can't wait to see how this one is gonna mess up your world."

"Betty, don't say that," Mary said. "Jerry's gonna be a fine daddy."

Betty slammed her bedroom door. Mary looked to Jerry and clenched her jaw. "I don't know why you have to get her started like that."

Jerry did not want to argue with his mother. "I guess I'll go out and see what Andrew's doing."

Behind the house, Jerry found Andrew equipped with a mattock, shovel and wheelbarrow to go with the rake. Wearing gloves, jeans and a dark hoodie, Andrew worked the ground, creating a flat, clear space where they would eventually build a fenced-in turkey run.

"Starting to look good back here," said Jerry.

"Think so?" Andrew looked to his uncle with pride.

"Yeah. We didn't see you at the fireworks. You missed a good show."

"Naw, I was here all night."

"Did you get here right after we left? Cause I didn't see ya all day."

"I guess. I don't know." Andrew pulled his phone from his pocket and checked the time. "Did the fireworks just get over? It's awful late."

"No, we went up to Calhoun's after. Mom brought you and your mom some pie."

"What kind?"

"It's a surprise."

Andrew stepped out of the shadows and Jerry saw

43

his face for the first time. "Did somebody hit you?" Jerry asked.

"What do you mean?"

"Your eye. It's awful red."

Andrew thought about it and said, "A bug flew in it, and I've been rubbing it."

"A bug did that? Must have been a big bug," Jerry said and stepped toward Andrew to look at his eye.

"Yeah, it was a big one," Andrew said. He stepped away from his uncle, preventing him from getting a closer look. "I probably made it worse rubbing on it."

"So, what are you thinking back here?" Jerry asked. "Looks like you've about got it ready to start building. Do you know what you're gonna do?"

"Naw. I was just smoothing it all out. You said that was the first thing we needed to do, get the ground all smooth and flat."

Jerry walked over the space, sliding his foot to emphasize the even ground. "That's right. Get it any better, and we can pave it to put up a parking lot."

"There was some bad rocks in there," said Andrew. "But I got them out pretty good, huh?"

"Yeah, you did."

Andrew's turkey project was launched through the efforts of his grandmother. After speaking to Preacher Bryant about her grandson's problems, Mary found a website for helping people deal with addiction. The advice said to keep the person busy, active and engaged. Often, the troubled individual simply has an addictive personality, and transferring their focus away from something harmful is the key to recovery. When Mary and Jerry presented this to Andrew, he asked if he could raise turkeys. Mary and Jerry thought it was a great idea. It would require daily feedings, clipping wings, gathering eggs and maintaining a clean home for them. Jerry would help him get started, but Mary made Jerry agree that he could only offer help. This would be Andrew's project and his responsibility.

"Got an extra set of gloves out here?" Jerry asked. "That big piece of pie I had has got me all fired up to work."

"What kind did you have?" his nephew asked.

"Same as you're going to have."

"And what's that gonna be?"

"Oh, you think you're gonna outsmart Uncle Jerry, huh? I aint gonna ruin the surprise. But it sure was awful good."

Andrew smiled. He pointed to the metal shed where the lawnmower was stored. "I believe there's another pair in there."

Jerry stepped into the shed and came out wearing gloves. He carried a set of post hole diggers and a long steel bar with a pointed end. He walked to one corner of the space Andrew had cleared.

"This where you're gonna have the lot start?" Jerry asked.

"Yeah, if you think that's right."

Jerry nodded. He dropped the steel bar and slammed the post hole diggers in the ground to scalp the top of the dirt.

"You reckon we can get the turkeys this week?" Andrew asked.

"The feed store only has them on Thursday mornings. We will have to wait until next weekend, cause you won't have this ready for them tomorrow."

"Oh," Andrew said, disappointed. "So, eight days then?"

Jerry slammed the post hole diggers again and pulled

a big chunk of dirt from the ground.

"Unless you want to get the fence up tonight," Jerry said.

"Just the fence? That all we need."

"Yeah, we can build the house later. They will be so small, you can put them in a large Rubbermaid with a light for a few weeks. We got one of them in the shed. But you're gonna want to let them out to run around some, and you have to have the fence done for that. They can't live in a box all the time."

"We can do that tonight?" Andrew asked eagerly. "The fence part?"

"Don't know why not. You and mom can go down in the morning and pick them out."

Jerry slammed the post hole diggers again and grimaced. "But boy that's some rocky dirt. Grab that bar there."

Andrew picked up the steel bar. "This?"

"Yeah," Jerry said. "When I pull the dirt out, you jab that pointed end into the ground and bust it up for me."

Andrew tried to hold the bar over his head like he was preparing to throw a spear.

"It'll take both hands," Jerry said. "And you gotta hold it straight up and down."

Andrew put his second hand on the bar and held it perpendicular to the ground. "Like this?"

"Yep. Now jab it down in there," Jerry pointed toward the spot.

Andrew held the bar up high and stabbed down toward the hole, but the heavy bar got away from him. It slid out of his upper hand as he pushed down. He missed the mark by several inches.

"Here, you take the post holes and I'll do the bar,"

Jerry said.

"Okay, I know how to use them," Andrew said, willingly. "I've done that before. I don't know how you do that bar thing, but I know how to use these."

"Good."

Andrew took the post hole diggers from his uncle. He heaved them into the hole Jerry had started but did not retrieve any dirt.

"I told ya," said Jerry. "Nothing but rocks. Let me use the bar and bust it up for you."

Jerry stabbed the hole with the metal bar, breaking the rocks and dirt. He pierced the ground again and again, each time swirling the bar in the broken mix. "Now try it," he said to Andrew.

Andrew plunged the post hole diggers into the ground and pulled out a full load of soft, broken dirt and rocks.

"There you go," said Jerry.

Andrew dropped the dirt into the pile Jerry had started and stepped back to let his uncle jab the hole with the bar again. They developed a rhythm, three punches with the bar, followed by the thump, clang and dump of the post hole diggers. Jab, jab, jab, thump, clang, dump. The metal, earthy tune filled the quiet night. Jab, jab, jab, thump, clang, dump. After seven circuits of their tasks, Jerry stepped back and said, "That one looks pretty good. Three more holes and we'll be ready to set them posts."

*　　　　　*　　　　　*

The clock on the kitchen stove read 1:42 as Jerry made his way through his dark trailer and into the bedroom. He stripped off the dirty pants and shirt he wore while working with Andrew. The white t-shirt underneath was soaked through with sweat and stuck to his body. He pealed it off and tossed it on the floor of the bedroom and stepped toward the bed.

"You are not getting in this bed without showering," Susie's voice cut through the darkness.

"I thought you was asleep."

"I was, until I dreamed a billy goat came walking into my bedroom."

"I don't smell like a billy goat," Jerry protested.

"That's what a billy goat would think," she answered.

Jerry pulled up the blanket to get in the bed. Susie kicked her leg over to his side and stuck her foot up to prevent him from laying down. "Jerry Somerset, I aint kidding. You get in the shower before you crawl in here."

"Seriously?"

"Seriously."

Jerry stepped into the adjoining bathroom, the three-quarter design with only a stand-up shower. He turned on the water and stepped back into the bedroom. "Letting it warm up. Happy?"

"Yes, but I will be even happier if you pick up them clothes while you wait."

Jerry collected his dirty clothes from the floor and tossed them in the basket in the bathroom.

"Did you ever ask your mom if she knew what Geneva was wanting for her parents' house?" asked Susie.

"Naw, I aint thought to bring it up. I figured with the baby coming, we wouldn't wanna be thinking about buying a house right now."

"We certainly wouldn't wanna move away from your

48

mom, now would we?" Susie asked.

Jerry ignored her deeper implication. "It's not that. We just don't have it right now."

"But you heard that feller tonight. People think you'll be sheriff next."

"I don't know."

"I was looking online just now and I saw--"

Jerry interrupted, "I thought you said you was going straight to bed."

"Well, I tried, but that feller tonight made me think, so I looked online and saw that the starting salary for a sheriff in Kentucky is seventy-five thousand dollars. Did you know that?"

"Yeah. Everybody knows that."

"Well, I didn't."

"Plus," Jerry said, "there's that tax thing too."

Susie continued, "Right, there's an extra amount you get from the county property tax, so seventy-five is low for what you'd make."

"I know all this," Jerry said. "I've always known this."

"How in the world do you know all of this, Jerry, if you don't seem more determined to get that job once Danny wins the election?"

"Who says I aint determined?"

"You just don't seem like it. You could be pushing harder, telling folks you wanna do it."

"Everybody knows I wanna be sheriff, but I aint gonna nag over it."

"That's so much more money, baby."

"Yeah, it is. Like more than twice as much as what I make now."

"Twice as much? Do you even know what you make now? You made twenty-six thousand, six hundred and forty-two dollars last year. So, with that base sheriff salary plus the property tax bonus, your salary would more than triple."

"That's a lot."

"Uh, yeah. More than enough for us to buy Geneva's house."

"But I aint sheriff yet."

"If they don't give it to you this time, and Lord only knows who they got in mind now, then after the baby, I could go back to the dollar store part-time, and we could--"

Jerry interrupted, "You said you wouldn't want to work until she starts to school."

"I know. But I don't want her growing up here neither. She needs a house, Jerry. Not this place."

Jerry sighed.

"You're letting all the water run out," Susie said.

"Yeah, I guess I should get in there. You wanna join me?"

"Oh my God. Jerry Somerset, you are something else. Get in there. And I will be asleep when you come out, so you better be quiet."

CHAPTER 3

Me and Jerry's been married for seven years now. We've lived next to his mom and them all that time. Jerry found a cheap trailer to sit next to her house, and I thought that was the perfect place for us to be. I grew up with all kinds of aunts and uncles and cousins and grandparents right next to each other in the same holler, so I was used to everybody being on top of each other like that. Being in everybody else's business, you know. But after this many years, you start to want your own house and your own place in the world.

After high school, I started working at the dollar store. I thought I'd do it for a few years and eventually go to college. My friend Robyn's mom runs the dollar store, and she said I could work there. Once I started, she'd say I was the best worker she ever had. I think it was just because I didn't smoke like all the other ones, and I never had to take smoke breaks.

That year, Jerry started coming in when he was on duty, and things just went from there. I kinda knew of him, but he was quite a bit ahead of me in school. He was actually in the class with my brother. I'd see him at ballgames and didn't think much of him. He seemed to be a popular guy and all, but he didn't leave an impression on me back then. I wasn't into boys like him in school.

I remember the first time I saw he was a policeman; I couldn't believe it because my brother wasn't doing much of nothing at that time, and they was the same age. I even asked him about it. I said, "That Jerry Somerset is already a policeman and here you are smoking pot all day and don't even have a job."

"County deputy aint no job," he said. "He's just a glorified hall monitor."

I never knew why he felt that way about Jerry. That didn't make no sense, but like I said, my brother smoked a lot of pot back then.

At the dollar store, I got used to Jerry's routine. He'd come in every Tuesday and every Thursday at three o'clock. He'd always get a sleeve of cashews, some tater chips - those barbeque Grippos kind - and an Ale-8. The same thing every time and always at three o'clock.

I got to doing this little thing where I'd tell him the price before I rang it up. It embarrassed him at first. I think he likes to pretend that people don't notice him, but I noticed him. And I wanted him to know that I noticed him. So, as he'd come to the counter, I'd say, "$3.18, just like it was on Tuesday," and then I'd ring it up.

One day, and again this was just a few years after high school, so I didn't know no better, but one day, I got it on my mind that I wanted to have car trouble and have Jerry give me a ride home. I know how that sounds, and I don't know what I was thinking, but that's what I wanted. It was a Tuesday or a Thursday, but I wasn't working that day. I knew he'd be stopping in there at the dollar store at his usual time for his cashews and stuff, and as crazy as it sounds, it just bothered me that I wouldn't be there to ring him up. I didn't want nobody else to do it.

So, I went there to the dollar store, and I got there a few minutes before him. I went in, bought a few things and came out and pretended my car wouldn't start back. I knew enough about cars to pull my coil wire to keep the spark plugs from firing. I popped the hood and pulled that wire, taking it out real careful. I left it sitting on the connector, but I made sure it wasn't hooked up. Then I just sat there like I was all helpless and waited for Jerry to show up.

And sure enough, he pulled in right at three o'clock in that big shiny police car. I got a little flutter in my stomach because I knew what I was about to do. I wanted to ride in that car next to Jerry and hear that siren and see them lights, and I knew I wasn't about to rob a bank to get to do that.

He came right over to my car and said, "Hey Susie, you having trouble?" I believe that was the first time I ever heard him say my name. It was right there on my nametag all that time, but it took me being out of uniform for him to say it.

"Uh-huh," I said. "Don't know what's wrong." I tried to give him the saddest puppy dog eyes he'd ever seen.

"You mind if I try it?" he asked.

"Go ahead."

He hopped in the driver's seat and tried the ignition. He said, "Sounds like your spark plugs. Like they aint firing."

He came around and looked under the hood. I just stood there, like I didn't know nothing about nothing. He fidgeted a bit under the hood and then looked at me all confused and said, "Well, that's odd. Your coil wire is off, almost like someone just pulled it off. You didn't pull your wire out, did ya?"

He looked at me awful funny, and I must have turned every shade of red there is. I couldn't think of anything to say, so I just stood there like an idiot. Then you could see it on his face that he saw what I was doing. He turned a bit red hisself and then went back under the hood. He popped the coil wire back on and jumped in and started it right up.

"I think that'll do it," he said and then went off into the store. He looked back at me, again all confused, and he must have thought I was just plum crazy because I hadn't said thank you or nothing.

The next day I worked a Tuesday or a Thursday, he didn't come in at his normal time. I kept looking out the window, wondering if he'd show up, but he never did. I figured I'd run him off. But then at five, when my shift ended, I went out the back and Jerry's police car *was parked back there next to mine.*

His window was open and he said, "I'm off duty until six. I was thinking about running up to the dairy bar. Wanna go with me?"

I jumped in and away we went. We got us Stromboli sandwiches and onion rings, and then he brought me back to my car. On the way back, he asked if I wanted to turn on the lights and play with the siren.

And that was all she wrote, as they say.

*   *   *

Jerry entered his trailer through the kitchen door and saw Susie chopping a salad on the bar. Working on the radishes, she sliced them extra thin so the chips would curl at the ends. Jerry did not like radishes in salads, but Susie did. Jerry said a big chunk of radish overwhelmed everything around it. Any salad with radishes was essentially a radish salad. They compromised, and Susie agreed to include them only in tiny, thin slices.

"Looks like you're feeling good today," he said. "That late night out didn't bother you?"

"My feet hurt a little. Kinda swollen."

"I've been meaning to fix that garbage disposal for Mom," Jerry said, snatching a baby carrot from the ceramic bowl Susie used to collect the vegetables. He opened the refrigerator and pulled an Ale-8 from the door. He twisted off the top and drank. "I'll run over there right quick and do that before we eat. Is that okay?"

"You gotta go to the church and pick up Andrew."

"What?" Jerry said through the side of his mouth as he continued to drink from the bottle.

"Today's one of them meetings. Betty called and said

she couldn't get him."

"Why can't she get him?"

"She didn't say," Susie said, and smiled happily at Jerry.

"And you didn't ask her, I'm guessing?"

"I absolutely did not," she said and smiled even bigger. "I will not ask that woman her business. No sir."

"You're proud of yourself for that?"

"Yes, I am. I am very proud of that. Very proud indeed. People like your sister just want to drag you into their misery. If you don't ask no questions, you can pretty much stay out of it. I just say 'uh-huh,' 'yep,' 'okay, 'will do' and I don't end up in their messes with them."

"It sounds like you've actually thought all this through," Jerry said, studying his wife.

Susie beamed. "I have, and it works."

"I just can't do that though," Jerry conceded. "Not with her."

"No, you can't. That's your sister, and as long as we live beside her, I reckon you'll have to deal with her nonsense from now on."

Jerry sighed. "What time's he done?"

"Six-thirty."

"I got a few minutes. I could still change that--" Jerry began.

"No," Susie interrupted. "You'd be pushing it. You need to go get him. You need to be there when it's done. He don't need to wait around with them people after one of them meetings. Could get into all kinds of stuff."

"You're right," Jerry said. He hugged her from behind and wrapped his hands around her stomach. "What are you making with this?"

"Spaghetti. It'll be here when you get back. Now go get him."

*   *   *

Jerry pulled into the parking lot of the Mount Sinai Church. He exited his car and approached a sign on the door that read, "Recovery Through Christ: 5:00-6:30. All Welcome." Jerry heard Preacher Bryant inside, speaking to the group. He listened to the account of the Apostle Paul's Second Letter to Timothy, how believers can find strength and guidance in the Lord. "If you believe," the preacher said, "you will reign with Him, for no matter what you've done in the past, no matter how faithless you've been, He has always been there, waiting for you to turn back to Him."

Jerry walked a few steps into the church's corridor. He saw the group of eight people in a half-circle, facing the preacher. Jerry knew them all and had arrested most of them. Some looked at the floor, with their arms crossed. Blank expressions, waiting for this to be over. Jerry knew they were there only because they were required to attend. They would arrive, and for ninety minutes wish they were somewhere else. Their lawyers or probation officers told them it would look good on their record if they demonstrated a real commitment to change. Preacher Bryant could bear witness to an individual's redeemed heart in court and help carve months or even years off their sentence.

Not all saw him as a necessary path toward a lighter punishment, however. Some were there because they found sincere structure and meaning in his words. The session with Preacher Bryant would inspire them to rededicate their lives to their recovery. For the next few days after a meeting, they would quote him often. "Preacher Bryant said this," and "Preacher Bryant said that." Friends would quietly wonder if they had joined a cult. The newly inspired would occupy their free time with gardening, trying to find a job or reconnecting with relatives. They made promises to them that this was the time they really changed. And when they said it, they believed it to be.

They would feel that burst of encouragement from Preacher Bryant again when they were only two days away from the next meeting. They would use him as an excuse to follow the straight path. "If I take a drink today or smoke something or snort a pill, Preacher Bryant might ask me about it tomorrow, and I can't lie to that man," they would say.

But it was those days in the middle that were the hardest, and that is when they would cheat. Those days when they were three days past their last meeting with the preacher and still four days away from the next. The sweet call of relief or pleasure or warmth or safety that could only be found in a Xanax or a crushed Vicodin was too much to resist. On those days, Preacher Bryant was a fading memory, the angel who used to be perched on a shoulder giving good advice, but who was now in another room, speaking through a wall and giving muffled support.

But that Vicodin, it was there. And it called to its friends. It knew how sick they felt and it knew how to make them feel better.

"I just need something to calm my nerves," they would say. "Just this one today and then I'll be straight. I just need one. Just one."

Jerry saw Andrew looking at Preacher Bryant with genuine interest, even scribbling a note when he heard something he wanted to review later. Jerry saw this and smiled to himself, trying to remember to tell his mother about it.

The forty-five-year-old Preacher Bryant wore pressed jeans and an olive Patagonia fleece jacket that covered a collared dress shirt. Normally in a suit and tie, he tried to make these meetings more welcoming by dressing in what he considered his casual attire. With pedicured hands, salt-and-pepper hair and the golden July tan that he somehow wore all year, Preacher Bryant sometimes had to defend his carefully preened appearance to members of the community who thought he spent too much time looking in the mirror. When pressed on it, he would say hair spray and tanning beds were his only vices. He rationalized that his audience was more open to hearing his message if he looked his best, so he made an effort to do that every day. He would say, "If my hair is not in order or if I have a blemish on my face or if my jacket has a hole in it, people in the pews will focus on that flaw in me and not hear God's unflawed words. I can't have that."

Preacher Bryant saw Jerry in the corridor. He looked at his watch. "Oh, I've done it again, let the time get away from me," the preacher said. "I'm so sorry, I'll let you go in a minute, but before we close, I want to remind you of two of my favorite passages, Proverbs 6:27 and 28. They ask, 'Can a man scoop fire into his lap and not get burned? And can a man walk on hot coals and his feet not scorch?' That's Proverbs 6:27 and 28."

Andrew wrote the passages on his notepad.

"I want you to think about those two for next week, okay?" the preacher said. "We'll have some things to say about them."

The attendees gathered their belongings and filed out of the church. Preacher Bryant approached Jerry. "Good to see you, Jerry. How's Susie?"

"Oh, she couldn't be better."

"You two have to be excited. Whenever I see you in church, I can see it on your faces. What a blessing."

"We do feel blessed, thank you."

"Help yourself to a Danish. I had one earlier. They're awful good," Preacher Bryant said and motioned to a card table at the back of the room. On it was two stainless steel carafes of coffee and a plate of homemade cherry-cheese Danishes.

"Those look great," said Jerry, walking toward the card table. "You make them yourself?"

"I wish. Calhoun's sends something over every week. Ten minutes before we start, a car pulls up and one of the girls gets out with the coffee and a plate of whatever they threw together for us. I always tell them they will never top the previous week's goodies, but they somehow always do."

"Calhoun's?" Jerry asked. "They got Danish there?"

"I don't even know if it's on the menu, but usually what they bring isn't something they serve regularly. We never ask for it, but they always bring something. You can tell it's something they just like to make. Maybe trying them out on us, like we're guinea pigs."

"That's good to have here at these meetings," said Jerry. "Maybe that's why some people come, just for the desserts."

Jerry immediately regretted how that sounded. The preacher saw his unease and forced a chuckle to allow Jerry to relax.

"Maybe you're right," said the preacher.

"Reckon I can take one for Susie instead?" Jerry

asked. "She'd probably like one."

"Absolutely." The preacher smiled at Jerry. "I need you to come speak to some of my husbands who attend marriage counseling with us. I can't get some of them to think of anyone but themselves."

Jerry picked up two paper plates and carefully placed a large Danish between them.

*   *   *

"I plum forgot to look in on them," Jerry said to Andrew as they rode in Jerry's car. "How many did y'all get?"

"Six."

"Gave them food and water already?"

"Yep. They stayed under that light, all bunched together."

"Probably got cold when you brought them home."

"They aint big as nothing," Andrew said.

"I bet not, but they grow fast, I hear."

Jerry was unable to think of anything else to ask about the turkeys, but he wanted to keep the conversation going. "How's that back there?"

"What?"

"Back there at the church."

"The program?" Andrew asked.

"Yeah, how is it?" Jerry said. "Is it just a lot of preaching?"

"I don't know. It's all right, I guess."

"Is it going to work? For you?" Jerry asked.

"I guess," Andrew said. He put on his headphones and turned away from his uncle.

*   *   *

Jerry tightened the garbage disposal with an Allen wrench and slid from under his mother's sink. He returned her box of dishwashing pods and a bottle of ammonia cleaner to where they were when he began his work.

"Should be okay," Jerry said. "I'll get the power back on."

He left the room, and Mary walked to her stove to stir her pot of chicken and dumplings. The lights in the kitchen came on. Mary opened a cabinet and removed four dinner plates.

"That should do it," Jerry said, as he returned to the room.

"Sit down and have a bite," said his mother.

"I told you. Susie's cooking."

"Won't hurt just to have a couple," she said. "What's she making anyway?"

"Spaghetti."

"Lord have mercy, why would anyone want to eat such a thing? I guess I wanted strange stuff too when I was that way with you and Betty. But it never made me want nothing like spaghetti."

Mary sat a plate at the head of the table. On it was a small portion of dumplings and a chunk of cornbread.

"You can eat that much and still have room for that old stuff she's making," Mary said.

Jerry eyed it. "I'll try one of your dumplins, but then I gotta go."

Jerry picked through the plate and found one large dumpling. He forked it, blew on it, and ate it. Mary watched proudly.

"Need a little salt or pepper?" she asked.

"No, it's perfect," said Jerry. He forked around his plate for another one.

The front door opened, and Betty entered the house. She walked into the kitchen and dropped her keys and purse on the table.

"You got Andrew?" she said to Jerry. "Starla didn't have a ride home, and I had to take her."

"You have rides for your friends, but can't take care of your son?" Jerry said to his sister.

Betty glared at Jerry as she ladled dumplings on her plate. She added green beans and cornbread and sat beside her brother, continuing to scowl at him but not answering his question.

"Where is he now?" she finally asked Mary.

"Out back playing with his turkeys," Mary answered. "I yelled at him ten minutes ago to come in and eat."

"Y'all get them today?" Betty asked.

"Yep. Me and him went this morning," Mary said. "Got six of the cutest little things you ever saw."

Betty blew on her dumplings to cool them. "I'll go look after I eat."

Jerry stood and carried his empty plate to the sink.

"Looks like you took care of it all," said Mary.

"Sure was good," Jerry said. "I need to head on over before Susie comes looking for me. I'll check in on Andrew and tell him to come in."

Jerry left his mother's house and walked toward his trailer. He stepped back behind the house and saw Andrew shooing two turkey poults around the pen they had constructed the previous night.

"Supper's getting cold," Jerry called to him.

"I know."

"Come on in. Mom don't need to wait on you."

"Let me get these last two under the light."

Four of Andrew's turkeys were in the forty-gallon Rubbermaid container under a brooding light. He had two out in the run, letting them skip around and peck at the ground.

"Tiny little fellers, aint they?" Jerry asked as he stepped toward the turkey run. Aside from the brown on their heads and undeveloped wings, the Bourbon Red poults were the same color yellow as Mary's dumplings. And just as fluffy.

"Look at them run," said Andrew. "I can't hardly catch them they're so fast."

*   *   *

Susie sat across from Jerry at the kitchen table. Her dinner plate was empty, and she worked on the Danish Jerry brought her from the church.

"This sure is good," she said. "Thank you." She looked across and noticed Jerry was slow to eat the plate of spaghetti she had prepared for him.

"I know what happened," she said, pointing to his plate.

"What?"

"You filled up on these Danishes before you came home, didn't you? That's why you don't want none of my spaghetti."

"You know me so well."

The phone rang. Jerry answered and heard the voice of the police department dispatch officer on the other end. "You gotta get over to Stanley Jennings' house."

CHAPTER 4

They made me sheriff of this county when I was twenty-five years old. I know Daddy was awful proud of that. I took over the job from Sheriff Bolling. We aren't supposed to talk about him, but I'll say a little bit. He seemed to be doing fine in the job, and everyone said he was a nice enough feller, but some strange things started happening in the county with him in charge.

There was one time, one of his deputies had pulled over a car at the county line, and it was just plum full of dope. The deputy called Sheriff Bolling, but he also called the State Police. The state boy that came was David Moore. I went to grade school with him, and there's not a better man in the world than David. He always said he could not prove anything, but something awful strange happened with the sheriff and the dope that day. David said when they was all carrying bags of that dope out of the car, a bag of it dropped out of the sheriff's jacket, like he had it wedged against him with his elbow. The dope just fell right there on the ground in front of everybody. They all stood there looking at him, not knowing what to say.

The sheriff finally barked at his deputy, "Put it into evidence," and went on like nothing was wrong. Nobody could have proved anything, like David said, but it seemed to everyone that the sheriff was trying to steal dope right there in front of all of them. Not really even doing much to hide it.

You'd hear about them things when Bolling was sheriff. There'd be girls who got hooked on pills bad. People would say the sheriff would keep an eye out for them and pull them over. Not that they'd done anything wrong. But he'd start going through their cars, making threats and end up working out some kind of deal with them. You know what kinda deal I mean too. People said they heard stuff like that, but nobody really knew anything for sure, and it was always the word of one of those girls on pills against him, the sheriff.

So Deputy Somerset - that's Jerry, by the way - Deputy Somerset had heard enough of all these little stories. That was his boss, and he started feeling like everybody was holding it against all the men in uniform because the sheriff wasn't no count. He started to keep tabs on Sheriff Bolling, and he caught him in some awful bad stuff. Once he had all the information he needed, he went up to the restaurant one Thursday morning when Sheriff Bolling wasn't attending Daddy's meeting. They say Jerry just walked in uninvited and told Daddy and the mayor and the judge everything he knew about Sheriff Bolling. He had pictures and ledgers and receipts. Jerry had that old boy dead to rights. Daddy and them thanked Jerry for letting them know and then they called Sheriff Bolling in. By the end of that day, the sheriff was gone from Buckner County. Never came back neither. Last I heard he was working on a cattle ranch out in Nevada. Just as a hired hand.

Now Jerry might've thought he would be in line to be sheriff once that happened, and he probably did deserve it. There's times when I wouldn't be able to do my job without him. Like when we're heading into something real bad, and I make sure Jerry is there to go in first. Suicides, for instance. I hate walking into those scenes not knowing what I will find. And we have that way too often here in Buckner County, young people killing themselves. The drugs too. I can't keep up with all the drugs coming in from other states, but Jerry knows them right off. He recognizes particular kinds of methamphetamines that come from West Virginia or the names of pharmacies in Florida where people go down and get those pain pills.

So yeah, you could say Jerry is better at my job than I am, but I sure don't think that's why he turned Sheriff Bolling in. Daddy and them figured I'd be better for the job, and I know that didn't set exactly right with Jerry. But from my first day on, he's bit his tongue and done everything he could to help me.

*   *   *

Jerry talked to State Police Officer Arnold Buckhorn on the front porch of Stanley's house. "Wasn't he just in the hospital?"

"Yeah," agreed Buckhorn. "Knee surgery."

Many neighbors and family members had gathered in the driveway and front yard.

"Jerry, what happened?" one of them yelled from behind police tape.

Jerry shook his head.

"Did somebody kill him?" someone else asked.

"We'll see what we can find out," Jerry answered. "Y'all probably should head on home."

Officer Buckhorn motioned for Jerry to step inside with him and said, "His daughter told us she texted him this afternoon and he didn't answer. She assumed he was asleep, so she just stopped by on her way home from work and found him like this."

"He lived alone, right?" Jerry asked.

"Yeah, we can't find anybody that says they seen or talked to him after last night. The daughter said she stopped here before the fireworks."

"I saw her there," said Jerry.

Officer Buckhorn escorted Jerry into the kitchen. When they entered, Jerry saw Stanley's body propped up against the wall, his head leaned over on his shoulder. His eyes were still open.

"Just bled out," said the officer.

"Looks that way," said Jerry. He noticed the baptism picture above Stanley's body.

"My mom has that painting in her house," said Jerry.

"I've seen them in a lot of houses in this county," Buckhorn said. "That feller's local, right?"

"He is. I always liked this old man on the bridge here," Jerry said and pointed to a tall, slender figure in the painting. "He's in a nice suit and off by himself. I get the impression that he's not part of the congregation, but he's interested in what's happening in the creek."

"I guess I never looked at the thing that close," Officer Buckhorn answered. He looked back at the painting but saw Jerry had returned his attention to the body.

Jerry focused on the bloody smears above the left shoulder of Stanley. Written in brownish-red letters on the cream-colored painted wall was one clear word, "COACH."

"Coach," Jerry said to himself.

Above that word, Jerry saw two smears that also appeared to be words. The first one could have said "called" and the other one more clearly did say "me."

"Called…me…coach?" Jerry asked.

"That's what I see," said Officer Buckhorn. "I wanted to let you see it without hearing what I thought. But that's what I see too. A couple of the other fellers looked at it. One of them thought it said, 'caused me coach,' but that doesn't make sense. Everyone else sees what you see, although them two smeared words are awful messy."

"It definitely says 'Coach' though," said Jerry. "And

67

'me.'"

"Yep."

"Called me coach," Jerry repeated. He looked again at the blood trail from the bedroom. "That writing wasn't done by whoever killed him. He crawled from the bedroom and did that himself. The words, the blood, that's him."

"I'm with you on that," the officer agreed. "Was this man a high school coach or something?"

"No," Jerry said. "He was a barber."

"A barber?"

"Hey guys," another state policeman appeared in the kitchen. "Look at what I found in his office."

Jerry and Officer Buckhorn followed the man to another room in the house, the one Stanley used for his office. He had a desk with a computer, a whiteboard calendar and filing cabinets where he kept the records for the years he did the taxes for the barbershop. Diplomas were on the wall, along with certificates authenticating his barber and business licenses. One wall had a row of framed pictures, including one of a Little League baseball team. That team had sixteen young boys in two rows, dressed in their uniforms. Beside them was Stanley, smiling and proud.

"Coach," Officer Buckhorn said, pointing to Stanley in the picture.

"Coach," Jerry repeated.

They continued through the rest of the house. In the bedroom, Officer Buckhorn pointed to the empty gun case. "Medicine cabinet's cleaned out too," he said to Jerry. "Rest of the place looks untouched."

"We need to talk to his brother-in-law, Darryl Hoskins," said Jerry. "They was hunting buddies. He'll know what guns they took."

"That's Nancy Hoskins' husband? I believe I saw them outside," said Officer Buckhorn.

Bert Tackett, a younger deputy who worked with Jerry entered the room. "Jerry, is your phone turned on?" he asked.

Jerry looked at his phone. "I'm not getting any signal."

"Little Dan's trying to get up with you."

"That's Sheriff Calhoun," Jerry said, correcting the deputy.

"Right, I know, sorry," the deputy said. "Sheriff Calhoun wants to talk to you."

"I'll go call him from the car," Jerry said. "Can you find Darryl Hoskins outside and see if he can tell you what guns Stanley owned?"

"Yeah, I'll do that," Deputy Tackett said. "I mean yes sir, I'll go do that, sir."

"Tackett," Jerry stopped him.

"Yes? I mean yes, sir?"

"I'm the same as you. Don't call me 'sir.' There's no need for that. Sheriff Calhoun is your superior. Our superior. Respect his position."

"Yes, sir. I mean okay, Jerry."

Jerry went to his cruiser and talked to the sheriff on the radio. The murder investigation would belong to the Buckner County Sheriff's department unless they requested help from the Kentucky State Police.

"Let's see if we can run with this, Jerry," Little Dan said. "No need to get them boys involved."

"They're already here," said Jerry.

"I know that, but if you tell them we are handling things, they won't turn this over to their detectives. They're basically working for us tonight and then they'll leave unless we ask them to hang around."

"We don't want their help?" Jerry asked.

"Case like this involves a popular citizen and beloved member of the community. I don't think I have to tell you it will be good for me if my department figures this all out, and it will be good for you if you take the lead."

"I can do that," Jerry said.

"This is how careers are made," Little Dan continued. "People won't remember the day-to-day work you've done for twenty years, but they will remember that you were the man who put the handcuffs on whoever killed Stanley Jennings."

Jerry walked back to the house and saw Officer Buckhorn waiting for him on the porch.

"I just spoke to the overnight captain," Buckhorn said. "This will go to Detective Cross, but he won't be here until in the morning."

"We're going to keep this in house," Jerry said.

"You sure?"

"Yeah, I just spoke to the sheriff."

"He putting you in charge?"

Jerry nodded.

"They'll love to hear that. We've got missing persons who are probably dead, people burned alive on strip mines and one whole family that someone wants us to think died by accidental gas leak. Our detectives are stretched awful thin."

Deputy Tackett returned carrying a notepad. He held it out between Jerry and Officer Buckhorn.

"Give it to this man here," Buckhorn said, putting his hand on Jerry's shoulder. "He's the one in charge."

Tackett handed the note to Jerry and said, "Darryl says a 12-gauge pump Remington and a .30-06 Winchester with a scope. Said he slept with a thirty-eight."

"That's what y'all found in the yard?" Jerry asked Buckhorn. "A Smith & Wesson thirty-eight?"

"That's the one."

Jerry completed the handoff of the case from the state policemen on the front porch and went back into the house. Officer Buckhorn and his colleagues agreed to help disperse the crowd, but they left the county deputies alone in the home. When Jerry arrived in the bedroom, he saw Deputy Tackett staring at the empty gun cabinet.

"This just don't make sense," said the young deputy to Jerry. "We're looking at what, a couple hundred dollars from them guns? And a couple more for them pills, maybe?"

"Maybe more than that; depends on what the doctors gave him," replied Jerry. "Get a lot for a bottle of pills these days."

"Still don't seem like that's worth it to kill a man," said the officer.

"If you gotta have it," said Jerry.

"What do you mean?"

Jerry thought about it. He stepped back into the kitchen and looked at Stanley's body under the baptism painting and the trail of blood leading back to the bedroom. He finally said, "I arrested this guy once. On the way to jail, I was telling him about ways to get clean. He asked me if I went to church, and I said, 'Yes.' He claimed he didn't need to go no more, cause with four or five Demerol, he could talk to God face-to-face."

*   *   *

Jerry sat at his desk at the police station, entering details from the crime scene into his report template. He typed the words "pills" and "guns" and "blood" and "coach." Little Dan approached his desk, but Jerry did not see him reading the report over his shoulder.

"I never thought I would see bloody words on a wall written in a report," Little Dan said, and Jerry turned to see his boss watching him.

"It wasn't as bright as I would have expected," Jerry said. "You'd think something like that would stick out, but it looked a lot like someone with muddy hands had just touched the wall by accident. But then when you looked at it close, it was obvious that wasn't mud."

"And not by accident," Little Dan added.

"No, not by accident."

"There's been a million calls on Stanley this morning," Little Dan said. "The town wants a hanging."

"I can imagine," Jerry said. "You'll never hear anybody say a bad word about Stanley."

"Everything looks like a robbery?" Little Dan asked.

"I'd say so. And he ended up shot with his own gun. Probably over-estimated his skills as a vigilante."

"I talked to the coroner just a few minutes ago," the sheriff said. "We won't get that report for a while, but he said Stanley had probably been dead about a full twenty-four hours when y'all bagged him."

"And his daughter had seen him the previous evening when she went to the fireworks," Jerry added.

"Right."

"So he had to get killed right after that," said Jerry. "Probably when the rest of the county was listening to them Combs boys."

Little Dan nodded in agreement and asked, "But why 'Coach?' Why would he write that on his wall?"

"Here's what I'm thinking," Jerry turned away from

his desk and looked to his boss.

"Let me hear it," Little Dan said, pulling up a chair.

"The guy who killed him called him 'Coach' and that seemed odd to Stanley. So he thought it was important to tell us that detail."

"Why's that important? Why would it be odd to Stanley?"

"Because there's only a handful of people in the world who would call him that. Every day of his life, he'd hear people call him 'Daddy' or 'Stanley' or 'Papaw' or 'Mr. Jennings' or lots of other things. But not 'Coach.' Every now and then, however, he'd run into one of the players he coached many years ago, and it never failed that those boys – men now – still always called him 'Coach.' They called him 'Coach' just like they did when they were twelve years old and just like they've done every time they've seen him since. And they are the only ones who called him that."

"One of his former players then?" Little Dan asked.

"That's what I'm thinking. I bet the old man liked running into those boys as adults and still having them call him 'Coach.' Probably didn't think he'd hear it in a situation like that."

"I expect that's right," Little Dan agreed. "Any idea how long ago he did that?" Little Dan asked. "How old would them boys be now?"

"We saw one picture in his office. It said 2007 on it."

"So, them boys are in their early twenties now?"

Jerry nodded.

"Figures. That's the right age for peak stupidity."

"I was thinking the same thing."

Little Dan thought about it. "I bet if you head down to the newspaper office, they'd have old team pictures from those years. I know Eddie always does that one big page every year with all the teams and all their names."

*　　　　　*　　　　　*

The Buckner County Times called itself "The Voice of Troublesome Creek," allowing that moniker to reflect the waterway that splits Buckner County and is often the primary reference point for anyone giving directions. "You know where Troublesome Creek passes under that old wooden bridge? Well, my house is half a mile past there," people would say.

For the last forty years, the weekly newspaper claimed it flowed information through the county as essential as the water passing through the Troublesome. Not just wedding and death notices, community bulletin boards or classifieds; the paper also employed a handful of talkative, engaged ladies who wrote about the happenings in their communities. They informed readers about who hosted a family reunion, which lucky sports fans traveled to Cincinnati to watch a Reds game or what newlyweds just returned from Myrtle Beach.

The paper had yearly special pull-out sections, one for all the seniors graduating from Buckner County High School, another for candid photos taken at the county fall festival and one that detailed all the Little League teams in the county, showing their team pictures and posting the names of each roster.

When Jerry arrived at the office, owner and editor Eddie Phelps knew the details of the crime and had also determined the bloody words on the wall meant that Stanley was killed by one of his former players.

"Let me guess," said Eddie. "Killed by a guy who thought he should have been the shortstop all those years ago?"

"I think you got it solved," Jerry said, smiling. "We gotta put you on the payroll. So really, what do ya got?"

"Stanley coached five seasons, 2006 to 2010," said Eddie. "My boy played on the 2006 team. They won the county that year." Eddie flashed the team picture to Jerry. "That's him right there, Eddie Junior. I'm having him write a piece to put next to the obituary."

"That's a good idea," said Jerry. "Most people won't remember Stanley working with kids. Everybody just knows him from the barbershop."

"Right, we're gonna talk a lot about how he started his own business, and we have a real good picture of him cutting Joe B. Hall's hair in the 1980s," Eddie said, referring to the former coach of the University of Kentucky basketball team. He held that picture for Jerry to see.

"Huh, I've never heard about that," Jerry said, looking at the picture of the Hall of Fame coach getting his hair cut in Stanley's barbershop. "Maybe that's where old Stanley got the itch to coach."

"Oh, good gravy, Jerry," Eddie said. "I had not thought of that connection. I will have to say that for sure in the article."

Eddie paused to write a note on a pad on his desk.

"I have to write something to go beside what my boy is writing. He can't write a lick. He sent me what he had earlier and used the word 'I' fourteen times in two hundred words."

"That's bad?" Jerry asked.

"Yes, very bad," said Eddie. "Frankly, I'm depressed and ashamed that he's my boy, writing like that."

"What are y'all going to say about how he actually died?" Jerry asked.

"Oh, we'll just say he tragically passed away. We won't mention anything about bloody walls and gunshot wounds."

"You won't mention any of that at all?"

"People don't want to hear about stuff like that, Jerry. And they don't need to hear about it neither. They need the time and the place of soup bean dinners and bake sales. That's why they buy the paper. Not to hear details about a man's murder."

"But this is an important man and we don't have killings like this in this county," Jerry said. "Of people like him."

"Everybody thinks they know how to run a newspaper," Eddie said and gave Jerry a look that let him know the topic was not going to be discussed further.

"So, do you have those other team pictures I could look at?" Jerry said, after an uncomfortable pause.

"Yeah," said Eddie. "I know you're busy. The sheriff called me earlier and I got these out for you. Clippings for those teams. Names too."

Eddie pulled the files from a folder on his desk. He asked, "So seriously, you think it's one of these boys?"

"You know everything I know," Jerry said.

"Yes, I do."

"Let me ask you the same question," Jerry said. "Doesn't that make sense to you?"

"It does. It's heartbreaking to think he spent his last minute trying to pass you a message, but I do believe that's what he did."

Jerry skimmed the names of the boys in the first two photos, from 2006 and 2007. He saw the same photo that hung in Stanley's office. He looked over the 2008 photo next. When he looked at the 2009 team, Jerry froze. He dropped the other pictures to the desk and pulled the 2009 picture close to his eyes, studying one face on one little boy.

"What is it?" asked Eddie. "You see your killer?"

"My nephew," said Jerry. "I forgot he even played Little League. That's when he was living with his daddy's family."

"Which one is he?" Eddie asked.

"This one here," said Jerry. "Andrew Eldridge. He was going by 'Eldridge' then on account of his daddy's people."

"That's the Eldridges from Vicco?" asked Eddie.

"Yeah, that's them."

"That's a bad bunch, I hear," said Eddie. "His father's family."

Jerry nodded. He looked at the picture, saying nothing.

"You're close to that boy, huh?" Eddie continued.

"I am now," said Jerry. "I didn't see much of him that year when he lived with them folks. He was staying with an aunt and grandmother over there. His dad come and went, I understand."

"He's been in some trouble, aint he?"

"Sure has," Jerry said. "Nothing like this though."

"Well, there's lots of other boys that could be your man," said Eddie. "I see four or five in that photo you're holding that would cut their granny's throat for whatever you have in your pockets right now."

"They wouldn't get much," said Jerry.

"Like this little guy here, Clyde Bowling," Eddie said.

Jerry and Eddie looked at the benign, smiling twelve-year-old Clyde Bowling. A big chew of pink gum in his teeth, his freckled cheeks peeling from a sunburn.

"Yeah, he's bad news today for sure," said Jerry.

"Wouldn't know it back then, would you?" said Eddie. "Looks like a little guy you'd like to take fishing. But sometimes, they just don't grow up the way we want."

Jerry hung on Eddie's words, looking down at Clyde's sunburned face and then over to Andrew again.

*   *   *

Two years earlier, a windstorm knocked over the old smokehouse on the property of the Widow Jackson. She lived in the same holler as Jerry and had not used it as a smokehouse for years. When the structure fell over, the old woman had no plans for the pile of boards and tin, so she left them laying and ignored the blight out of her back window.

The following spring, when she walked past the pile on her way to her broccoli plants, she saw a rattlesnake resting under the shade of one of the bigger pieces of metal. With the walking stick she had carved out of an ironwood limb, the Widow Jackson took several swings at the poisonous snake, but it slithered away from her blows and hid under the boards.

Word of the encounter traveled fast down the holler, and when Mary heard about the snake, she sent Jerry and Andrew to help the old woman.

"Aint you gonna get your gun?" Andrew said to his uncle when Jerry handed him a metal rake.

Jerry held a hoe in his hand. "If two farm boys with artillery like this can't handle a single snake, we might as well move to the city."

"We're not farm boys," Andrew protested.

After the Widow Jackson showed them where she last saw the snake, Jerry had Andrew carefully begin to overturn each board and piece of tin with the rake. Once Andrew lifted a side off the ground, Jerry pried and poked under the raised boards and metal with the head of the hoe.

As Andrew raised one ashy gray inch board, he dropped the rake and jumped away from the pile. "There it is," he said. "I see it."

"Well, you don't want to go dropping your only weapon," Jerry said. He retrieved the rake and handed it to Andrew.

"I'll kill it," Jerry continued. "But you'll have to raise the board so I can get to it."

Andrew held the rake close to his chest. "I don't know," he said.

"I'm gonna be the one in danger," Jerry said. "All you gotta do is hold up the board for me."

Andrew agreed and crept around to the other side of the board. He looked to his uncle and saw an encouraging nod. Andrew stretched the rake over the board and caught the left side, pulling it up like a car trunk opening. Jerry saw the timber rattler coiled underneath.

"Pull it up a little higher," Jerry whispered.

Andrew pulled the board off the ground, and the big snake hissed at Jerry.

"Don't pay no attention to me, you pretty thing. I'm just here to say hello," Jerry said to the snake. He reached the hoe toward the serpent, letting it see the shiny red head. The snake sprung, lunging at Jerry and the tool. In one movement, Jerry stepped back, let the rattler extend itself out to its full thirty inches and came down with a clean blow from the hoe, detaching the reptile from its head.

The snake's body twisted into knots before it

stopped moving.

"You boys get it?" the Widow Jackson called from her porch.

"We got her, Miss Jackson," Jerry said.

Andrew stepped toward the snake, watching the tongue of the disembodied head twitch.

"Aint it dead yet?" Andrew said, prodding it with the rake.

"It's dead, but be careful. They can still bite you," Jerry said. "Still have the poison in them."

The Widow Jackson asked Jerry if he and Andrew would burn the boards to prevent other snakes from making a home there, but Jerry proposed instead they would take everything away for her. She agreed, and Jerry and Andrew took all that was left of her building. They stacked everything in the lawnmower shed at Mary's house, putting it off the ground on cinder blocks so snakes would not nest under them.

The boards and tin rested on the cinder blocks undisturbed for two years, but now Jerry and Andrew used them to build a house to shelter Andrew's turkeys. With what was salvaged from the smokehouse, Jerry identified boards for joists, floorboards, rafters and siding. Jerry used metal snippers to trim the pieces of tin to fit the roof on the little turkey house, and he fastened a door with a pulley, latch and spring mechanism so Andrew could leave the turkey door open during the day and close it at night. The spring slammed the door with enough force that a curious raccoon could not pry it open if it smelled a few easy meals roosting inside.

All that was left of the house was to put the metal pieces of roof on top. Jerry set the sheets of metal on the little house, overlapping them by an inch. He stood on the left side and hammered roofing nails through the tin. Andrew watched his uncle work before picking up his own hammer to begin driving nails on the right side.

"Wait just a minute," Jerry said.

"I can do it," Andrew said. "I can drive these things." He concentrated on trying to hit the first nail with a solid blow, his tongue sticking out through his pursed lips.

"I know you can do it," Jerry said. "But we have to chalk it first."

"Chalk it?"

"Yeah," Jerry said. "So it's a straight line all the way across. Each row of nails, in a straight line. I'm just getting the first row down now, but we'll need to chalk it before we drive the rest."

Andrew stepped back and looked at the roof.

"But why?" he asked.

"A real carpenter always puts their roof nails down with straight, chalked lines," Jerry said.

"But this is a turkey house. Nobody's going to see it. And we aint carpenters."

"Well, it looks better for one thing. But more important, there's right ways and wrong ways to do everything, Andrew."

"And you always do the right thing?"

"No, but I try. And not as a way to be all high and mighty neither if that's what you think. There's usually good reasons for doing things the right way, Andrew. And people who take shortcuts, they don't get ahead in the long run. They just think they do."

Andrew thought about that. He looked at his uncle and said, "What do you mean by 'chalk it' anyway?"

"You've never made a chalk line?"

"No, I guess not."

"Oh well, you're in for a treat."

Jerry retrieved the chalk box from the shed and showed his nephew how to mark straight lines for their nailing pattern. He let his nephew drive the nails and gave encouragement as the young man struggled to hit each head with balanced, straight blows.

"Good, that's a good one," Jerry would say, or, "That's okay, pull that one out and start over," if Andrew tried to correct a nail too crooked to uncurl.

When Andrew finished the last nail, he stepped back and admired his work.

"Now, don't that look good?" Jerry said. "Look at them straight lines."

Andrew smiled.

The two introduced the turkey poults to their new home and returned all the tools to the shed. As Jerry dropped the two hammers into the toolbox, he realized this time with Andrew had been an ideal opportunity to talk to him about the night Stanley was killed. He looked at Andrew and asked, "Do you ever see that King girl you used to bring over to the house all the time?"

"No, why?"

"I don't know. She looked awful cute at the fireworks the other night. Just wondering why you don't see her no more."

Andrew said nothing.

"Didn't you see her in that American flag t-shirt? Awful cute girl, that's for sure."

"No," Andrew said and looked to Jerry.

"You didn't? Come on, how could you not see her?"

"I wasn't there," Andrew said.

"Oh yeah, that's right," Jerry said. "You weren't there."

"No."

"You were here, right?" Jerry tried to pass off the question as if he just thought of it.

Andrew stopped him. "What are you doing?" he asked.

"What do you mean?" Jerry said.

"Why are you asking me this?"

"I was just talking about that girl you used to date, wondering why you never--"

"No," Andrew interrupted. "You weren't. You're trying to pretend like that's what you want to talk about, but it's something else."

Jerry said nothing.

"What are you trying to ask me?" Andrew said.

"I was just curious why you'd miss the fireworks. Where you could be."

"I was here, like I said."

"Okay, you were here," Jerry said.

Andrew looked around the shed. "Did we get everything put up?"

"Yeah, that should do it."

Andrew walked out of the shed. Jerry watched his nephew go inside the house. After he was gone, Jerry looked at the ground in the turkey run and thought about the work Andrew had done the night of the fireworks. How long would it have taken to clear that lot? Between the time Stanley's daughter last saw him the night he died and the moment Jerry returned with Mary and Susie from Calhoun's restaurant was almost five hours, more than enough time for Andrew to have been at Stanley's house and returned home to do that amount of work. And why was he so interested in working late that night? It was like he was establishing an alibi. But why? Jerry asked himself these questions as he finished in the backyard and made his way to his trailer.

When he entered, he saw Susie at the kitchen table, reading her phone and beaming.

"People's been messaging me left and right on Facebook all day," she said proudly. "Everybody knows you're in charge of finding this killer, and they want to know everything you're telling me."

"I hope you're saying I don't tell you anything."

"I am, but they also know I'm smarter than you and can get information without you knowing it."

"Oh yeah?"

"Yep," she said. "Everybody knows that."

Susie thumbed out a response to someone on her phone and grinned at Jerry as she typed.

"This is so fun," she said. "Everybody thinks I'm keeping secrets from them."

"Maybe this isn't supposed to be so exciting," Jerry said.

"Because that old feller's dead? I know, that's just awful."

"It's not just that somebody's dead," Jerry said. "Also, think about the family of the person we're gonna arrest. Or people. It could be more than one."

Susie stopped typing and looked at him. "Oh yeah." She paused and said, "Do you know who it's gonna be?"

"No, but I wouldn't tell you if I did."

"I know."

"But once we do have somebody, it won't just be their life that will be destroyed. Seems like the guy who killed Stanley Jennings is going to hurt a lot more people before this is over."

CHAPTER 5

Now Jerry's my brother, and I'd do anything in the world for him,
but sometimes he's a little hard to take. And don't get me started on
that wife of his. From the first time she came to our house, you could
tell she's thought she was too good for us and has been trying to get
Jerry away from us ever since.

There was a time when me and her both worked at dollar stores.
She worked at the one where everything costs exactly one dollar, but I
work at the one where things could be two or three or whatever
dollars. You could always get better stuff at my store, and everybody
knows it's better to come to ours unless they're just plain broke.
You'll see people in that one-dollar store counting out change to buy
a quart jar of soup beans. That'll be their whole order.

Anyway, Jerry talked her into quitting that place when he got her
pregnant. I guess he thinks he's one of them old rich fellers from way-

back-when who lets his wife stay home and raise the babies, but he don't make enough money to do that. He's in for a shock when he starts trying to buy diapers and formula.

We've got some good bulk deals on formula at our store. I've been telling him to come in and stock up, but they aint got much cabinet room in that trailer, so he'll probably do a lot of buying as they need it.

We've got a lot of stuff for babies and kids, especially school supplies. We got this thing worked out at our store where all the teachers in the county send us a list of the stuff their kids will need in their class. Paper, pencils, calculators, all them things. We've done that for years, where them Mommies and Mamaws would come in and say, "My kid has Mrs. Williams in third grade" and we could tell them exactly what they'd need.

After we did that for a few years, one of them women that works for Big Dan showed up the day after we got the list. I was the one working the register that day. She came up to me and said she wanted to buy everything on the list.

I said, "But I need to know which kids you want to buy for."

And she said, "All of them."

I asked her, "All of what kids?"

She started reaching into that big old pocketbook and just said to me like it was nothing, "All of all the kids. And can we get them all backpacks too?"

I had to call the manager and we added up how much it would be. He used some kind of big math formula he figured out on the call. As soon as I told that woman, she started writing out the check. It was a little over forty thousand dollars. My eyes just about fell out of my head when I saw it written out like that.

Then everybody in the county heard that they could come to our store and get their free school supplies. It was a stampede, like being at the Wal-Mart on the first of the month when everybody gets their government checks.

We'd stay late and actually make up the backpacks with

everything already in them, so the parents and kids wouldn't have to hunt for what they needed. We figured out to do one of them assembly line things. We now do that every year, and I get overtime that week, as we stay late and fill up them backpacks.

You'd think everybody would be happy to get something free, but I'm telling you, they just about fight over who is on the backpacks they get.

Them women will come in there and say, "I thought y'all had them Elsa backpacks up here. Why aint there any more Elsas?"

I wanna say, "Damn, you getting it all for free. Everybody can't get an Elsa. Be happy it aint got Osama bin Laden on it."

*   *   *

Jerry opened a small collaboration room in the police station. The room had one abandoned metal desk, and empty bulletin boards covered the walls. A large wicker basket sat on a filing cabinet, full of office supplies like tape, notebooks and markers. Jerry thumbtacked the team pictures on one of the cork boards and wrote a list of the boys' names with a dry-erase marker on a panel next to it.

On the first team, Stanley had sixteen players. Jerry wrote them all out. Each season, Stanley would lose four or five of the names to the Babe Ruth League and gain that many new players to fill the spots. Jerry wrote each one down, occasionally pausing to consider if one of those now grown boys participated in Stanley's murder. By the time he was finished, Jerry had written thirty-two names on the board. Andrew was not on his list.

Jerry looked again at the 2009 team and focused on Andrew's name on the roster. He considered writing it on the board as well, but decided to put him aside and focus on the other boys. He hid that photo behind some folders in the filing cabinet and told himself to forget about Andrew possibly being involved.

"Right?" Jerry asked himself. "It'll end up being one of them other ones for sure."

As Jerry made notes next to each name, based on what he knew about the lives of the men now, his eyes kept betraying him. They searched for the filing cabinet in the corner. It was as if Andrew was in the room with him, watching Jerry work and judging him for not respecting the possibility that his nephew could have committed such a crime.

"You know I could have done it," Andrew would be saying from the corner of the room. "You didn't see me at the time Stanley died, did you? Where was I? Why aren't you putting me on that board? I belong up there. Put me up there."

Jerry thought about the oath he swore, the responsibility given to him by the community, and the trust placed in him by the sheriff. He knew omitting Andrew's name from the list of suspects would look suspicious to his boss or other deputies if they audited his investigation. What was he hiding? After a deep sigh, Jerry picked up a marker and wrote, "Andrew Somerset, aka Andrew Eldridge" at the bottom of the board. He stepped back and looked at his now complete list.

"I swear," Jerry said to himself. "You better not have done this."

He sat at the desk and looked at Andrew's name. Jerry knew it might fall to him to help his nephew again. He thought back to a day twenty years earlier when Mary asked him to go with her to his sister Betty's house. Betty was living at the time in the head of Big

Oaks Holler with Andrew's dad, Harles Eldridge. The two had moved into a house left abandoned when Harles' grandfather died, and the couple took their newborn baby Andrew with them. The old man had allowed the house to deteriorate in the last years of his life, and it fell in further disrepair before Betty and Harles moved in. Mary said the house was no place for a new baby like Andrew. The mold alone could kill him, but the young couple liked being far away from Betty's hovering mother and did not mind the stagnant water in the basement. They developed a walking pattern to avoid the collapsing floorboards beneath the stained woolen carpet, the kind of cheap surface that scratched and burned the bottoms of feet just by walking over it.

"If they work on fixing it up for the next few years, Betty and them will have a nice place," Mary conceded when they first settled into the house. "But that man of hers aint no count, so he sure aint gonna do no such thing. It will be just as bad when they move out as when they moved in, if not worse."

When Jerry and Mary arrived that morning, it was his first time visiting the house. Jerry noticed bags of trash spilling out of the garage and large pieces of vinyl siding missing from the outside walls. An old washing machine rusted in the front yard, next to a fish tank missing the bottom glass panel.

"Is that stuff always in the yard like that?" Jerry asked his mother as they walked to the front door.

In the middle of the day, the house was silent. Birds sang in the trees nearby, and an old hunting dog bayed across the next mountain. But no light from the house, no movement, nothing.

"Something's wrong," Mary said. "I just feel it."

Mary knocked on the door and heard nothing in

return. Jerry tried to stand on his toes and look through the window to the living room, bending his head to see around the lime green curtains pulled together and tucked behind the couch.

"Betty? Betty! Are y'all in there?" Mary yelled through the door. When she heard nothing, she banged harder and slapped the aluminum frame. The bottom of her rings cracked against the metal like a shot from a .22 rifle.

Inside, a sound. A baby crying. First a whimper, growing to screams.

"That's little Andrew," Mary said to Jerry, her voice quivering. "He's crying, Jerry. Little Andrew. Something's awful wrong."

Mary tried to redirect her feelings of fear and helplessness to rage and anger, but her emotions failed her, and she melted into tears. She looked to Jerry to do something, anything. He beat the door harder than his mother, but his strikes only made Andrew scream louder from inside.

"I'll go around and see if there's another way in," Jerry said, walking through the thorny weeds in what used to be a flowerbed.

"Can't you just knock this door down?" Mary said.

"I'll try if I can't find another way."

Jerry jumped over a wooden fence to access the backyard. The brown grass had gone to seed and swallowed up scattered parts from a car engine project abandoned years ago. Jerry found the backdoor. When he touched it, the door swung open into the dark, quiet kitchen.

"Anybody in here? I'm coming in," Jerry said, as he stepped into the house.

He only heard the cries of his nephew and the

muffled sounds of his mother from the outside. "Hello? Betty? Y'all home?" he said, as he stepped around the card table in the kitchen.

Jerry followed Andrew's cries and found the baby stomach-down on a wet, brown stain in the middle of a playpen. Andrew's body was cherry red and pulsed each time he released a scream. Jerry froze, unsure what to do. He touched the baby, but the weight of his hand intensified the screams.

"Jerry? Did you get in?" Mary yelled from the outside.

Jerry made his way to the front door. He opened it from the inside, and Mary dashed past him into the house. She raced to the playpen, snatched Andrew and took him to the kitchen, leaving behind a trail of soiled clothes as she stripped him.

"Oh my God, you are a mess," she said to the baby. "Mamaw's here now. It's gonna be all right."

Andrew's screams continued.

"I know, I know," she said. As she cooed encouragement to her grandson, Jerry saw fear in her eyes.

"Betty? Betty?" Mary called into the silent hallway. She turned to Jerry. "Go in yonder and see if you can find them two. Something's wrong, bad wrong."

Jerry left Mary washing Andrew in the sink and crept down the hallway, unsure of what he would find. He heard his mother sing to her grandson to stop the crying, her soft voice crooned the song about mockingbirds and diamond rings as he reached Betty's bedroom. The door was shut, and Jerry heard nothing on the other side.

"Betty?" he whispered and tapped on the door.

Mary stopped singing. She yelled, "You're gonna

have to holler at them, Jerry." The change in her voice's inflection launched young Andrew screaming again. "Mamaw's sorry, baby. Uncle Jerry is checking on your momma. Lord have mercy, what in the world has she been up to?"

Jerry turned the doorknob and peered into the room. Inside, Betty lay asleep in the arms of Harles. In the sagging bed, he was shirtless and showed age beyond his thirty-five years. His graying chest hair swayed in the breeze of the room's oscillating fan and partially blanketed the faded pink tattoo over his heart. The design an attempt at either of cartoon fox or a gargoyle.

Jerry's eyes found the prescription bottles on the nightstand. The pills were ones Jerry would know well in his future career as a sheriff's deputy. On that day, he had not heard of OxyContin. Back then, most people in Eastern Kentucky still called them, "Those new super cancer pills."

Harles had stolen the bottle from his dying aunt's medicine cabinet, and he and Betty had not fully respected their potency. They treated them like their preferred 10 milligram Lortabs, crushing and snorting three each. That mistake sent them both into a fifteen-hour catatonic state.

As Jerry approached the bed, he saw they were both breathing. He touched his sister's exposed foot and shook her.

"Mom?" Betty said, waking up and seeing Jerry through a haze.

"It's Jerry," he answered.

"Jerry? What are you doing here?" Betty said as she wrestled her arms away from Harles.

"Mom's here too," Jerry said, just as Mary entered the room.

Mary looked over the scene and the couple's condition. "Y'all just go back to sleep. Aint nothing but a couple pillheads," Mary said, as she walked out.

"Mom?" Jerry said, following her.

"Grab that swing there." Mary pointed to a motorized rocker in the corner of the living room.

"The baby swing?" Jerry asked.

"Yeah, we're taking it."

"Mom, we can't just take things," said Jerry.

"We most certainly can," said Mary. "I was the one gave it to them. And now I'm taking it."

Betty staggered into the hallway and walked toward the living room. She saw her mother put Andrew on her hip and throw a diaper bag over her other shoulder.

"What are y'all doing here?" asked Betty.

"I said to go back to sleep," said Mary. "We were just leaving."

"You aint taking him!" yelled Betty.

Mary didn't answer. She looked to her son and said, "Let's go, Jerry."

Betty lunged for Mary and Andrew, but Jerry got in between them. As his mother dashed out of the front door, Jerry saw Harles come out of the bedroom, still in his underwear.

"Babe, they're taking our boy," Betty said to the big man.

Harles forearmed Jerry to the floor and went after Mary and the child in the front yard. Upon seeing him, Mary began double stepping to the car. Harles stumbled and went down to one knee, just as Mary arrived at the car and struggled with the door. After getting up in the house, Jerry ran out the door after Harles with Betty behind him. Jerry caught the big man just as they both arrived at Mary.

"Jerry!" Mary yelled as Harles reached for her and the child.

Jerry clapped the big oaf on the back, and when Harles turned around, Jerry leveled him with one hard punch to the jaw. As Jerry completed the follow-through on his punch, he felt his sister wrap her arms around his neck.

"You aint taking my baby," she yelled.

Jerry reached around his sister's waist and pulled her to his body. He turned his hip and flipped her on her back. The blow knocked the wind out of her. As she coughed, Jerry looked to Mary. "Get in the back with him, Mom, and lock that door."

Mary did as she was told. Jerry slid into the driver's seat and started the car, all in one motion. He floored the accelerator and peeled away from the house as both Betty and Harles struggled to stand.

If Andrew was involved in the murder of Stanley Jennings, rescuing him this time would not be so easy. It would not be Jerry's place to do it either. If he really believed his nephew could have committed the crime, the appropriate action would be to pass the case off to someone else. He should call Little Dan into the room, show him the list of names and tell him he could not work the case. They would turn the investigation over to the Kentucky State Police, removing any notion of impropriety on the part of the county office.

As Jerry considered this action, he began looking through the other names. He spent the next several hours making phone calls, pulling files and searching databases. He added notes beside the names on the whiteboard. Next to two names, he wrote, "Dead." Next to another, he wrote, "Prison." Two names were now tagged with, "State Policeman" and another said,

"Navy: San Diego."

With each name he removed as a possible suspect, Jerry realized he was closer to considering Andrew's involvement.

As Jerry weighed that possibility, the door to the collaboration room opened. Little Dan stood at the door speaking to Deputy Tackett. "Get that fax over to Doyle before you leave, okay?"

"Fax? We have one of those? Nobody has showed me a fax," the young deputy answered.

"I'll help you," said the sheriff. He stuck his head into the room and said to Jerry, "Be back in a second."

Jerry looked at the board with Andrew's name at the bottom. He decided he would show the list to the sheriff when he returned to the room and suggest they reach out to the State Police to take over the case. As that decision settled in his mind, he was overtaken by a feeling of relief. He would not deal with what he feared came next for the person investigating this crime. He would not have to be the person to arrest Andrew if he was guilty and would not have to give the violent, gruesome details to Mary and Betty about how Stanley had died.

But this feeling dissolved into one of helplessness. As much as he did not want those duties, he did not want to grant that power to someone else either. A stranger should not question Andrew or inform Mary that her grandchild was a killer.

As Jerry heard the squeaks of the sheriff's shoes coming down the hallway, he grabbed an eraser and wiped Andrew's name off the board.

"Aw Jesus," Jerry said to himself, feeling powerless to resist that impulse.

As the steps neared the door, Jerry looked again at

the list and saw the faint outline of Andrew's name. The eraser had not completed his deception. To finish the job, Jerry spat in his hand and wiped Andrew's name away with his fingers. He was satisfied the removal was complete just as Little Dan walked through the door.

"So, where are we?" said the sheriff.

"I started with thirty-two names," said Jerry. "I've eliminated the ones with the green comments after them."

"This one that says 'college,'" said Little Dan. "Do you know where he's at? Close enough to drive home and hang out?"

"University of Florida," said Jerry.

The sheriff looked at the nine open names. He was closer in age to the men listed and more familiar with them.

"Cross him off," he instructed, pointing to one of the names. "It aint him. Or him," he said, pointing to another.

He looked over the names again. "And him; that's Eddie's boy. And this one here. That feller is about to be a preacher."

"Okay?" said Jerry, unsure how his boss could be so certain.

"No use wasting your time on those," said Little Dan. "These five that's left. Anything on them?"

"Nope," said Jerry.

"Well, I guess we know what we'll be doing next, huh? Let's go knock on some doors," said Little Dan. He pointed to the five open names. "We gotta pay a visit to Clyde Bowling, Benny Stone, Anthony Craft, Jimmy Gibson and Jack Ritchie. Do you have any preference where we start?"

"Let's go with this Craft boy. Couldn't find nothing

on him. It's like he disappeared a couple years ago."

*   *   *

The Crafts lived on a farm close to the Letcher County line. They raised chickens and cows and a few Toulouse geese that played in the small branch of Troublesome Creek that bordered their property. In the summer, when the Canada geese took up residency at the Buckner County Lake, a few ganders were lured to the Craft farm by the honks of the Craft's Toulouse females. They soon learned the error of their visit, as the farm's alpha gander was as big as a bulldog and just as protective.

"Look at that thing," Jerry said to Little Dan as he noticed the big gander in the creek after they arrived at the farm. "You couldn't pay me to jump this fence and go in there with him."

"He'd eat you alive for sure," Little Dan agreed.

"Oh, he's just a big sweetheart," a voice called to them from the cornfield. An elderly man with a hoe came out of the garden and approached the two men. "If you give him a few handfuls of corn, he'll be your best friend for life."

Jerry and Little Dan explained the purpose of their visit to the man and asked about his son, Anthony.

"Been up in Ohio a few years now," the man said.

"You ever speak to him?" Jerry asked.

"Not really," the man replied. "Aint got much to say to nobody who wants to live in Ohio."

Jerry looked to Little Dan.

"Them's awful queer folks up there, in Ohio," the man continued.

"The whole state?" asked the sheriff.

"You ever meet anybody from Ohio that didn't have something wrong with them?" the man asked.

"A few, I guess," said Jerry.

"Well, you must be lucky, because I aint done it," the man said. "Never thought I would have raised a boy who wanted to live in Ohio, but I guess I did."

They asked him more about the specifics of how long ago his son left Buckner County and persuaded him to provide what he had for current contact information.

After they were satisfied with the visit, Little Dan began toward their cruiser. Jerry turned to the man and said, "Well, if you see him or if you hear he's been back in town--"

"I won't see him," the man interrupted. "And I won't hear nothing. He don't think much of his people or of this place. Always thought he was too good for it. He's happy up there in Ohio, I reckon."

At the car, Jerry saw Little Dan making a note to contact the authorities in Ohio, but neither man expected that trail to lead anywhere.

Near the Craft farm was Rogers Holler, the last listed residency of Jimmy Gibson. Jerry and Little Dan traveled up the holler looking for the house labeled 210 Rogers. They continued a mile past a mailbox with 108 written on the side in a blue permanent marker, when the road began to narrow and worsen. Little Dan questioned the accuracy of their notes. He stopped the car on the one-lane gravel and mud road because the limbs and branches reaching over from both sides were scratching the shiny panels of the cruiser.

The men both got out and looked around. Ahead was a deep mudhole they did not want to enter. No electric lines were visible, and no sounds of life could be heard.

"I got no signal back here," Jerry said, looking at his phone.

"Me either," said Little Dan. "No way anybody lives past here. These directions must be wrong. We're the first people that's been back here in years."

Jerry pointed to a log next to the road. "I don't know. See that beech yonder?"

"Yeah," Little Dan said.

"Looks like that thing fell into the road and somebody cut it to get it out of the way," Jerry said, pointing to the other half of the log, resting in a ditch.

"So?"

"So, it's a fresh cut. That means people still live up here," said Jerry. "Sawed timber is one of the clearest signs of civilization."

"Well, if there is anybody up past here, they live beyond where the world ends. They'll be some awful strange folks."

Jerry looked at him and grinned. "Like people from Ohio?" he asked.

Little Dan laughed. "Exactly. Just like people from Ohio."

They stepped back toward the car, but Little Dan stopped and said, "What's that sound? You hear that?"

Jerry paused. Through the trees, he heard the soft strums of a dulcimer. The music opened simple and low, a slow pulse repeated to establish a rhythm. Then the architect of the sounds directed the dulcimer to soar. The picker worked the instrument to a delightful twang that sweetened the air around the two men. Just as they felt warm and safe in the music's unwavering embrace, the musician asked something else of his device. A longing, unfulfilled whine next filled the mountains, as Jerry and Little Dan stood frozen, listening to the world around them ache as told through the pitch and vibration of metal wire strings. The woods played a song just for them, and the sounds they heard were an absolute beauty, like God strummed them himself.

"Come on," Jerry said. "He must be that way."

They left the car behind and walked toward the sound. After a few steps, a cabin appeared, hidden from their view earlier by a cluster of white pine trees. Kudzu covered most of the structure's gray wood boards and a chimney made from brown creek rocks. The cabin fit snug inside the trees, with no yard or parking spot. It was as if it had fallen from Heaven and the trees grew up around it.

As the men stepped down the hill to the little home, they followed the music toward the back porch. Little Dan stepped between the pine trees on the side of the house and made his way to the back of the cabin. There on the porch, he saw Jimmy Gibson strumming his dulcimer.

"Excuse me, sir," Little Dan called to him, as Jerry joined them behind the cabin.

Startled, Jimmy answered, "How long you been there?"

"Long enough to know you play fine music," said Little Dan. "I don't know if we've met, but I'm Dan Calhoun. Are you Jimmy Gibson?"

"Yes, I am. I believe you're the sheriff," Jimmy said. "Heard your name, but never seen you."

"That's right. I am the sheriff. And this here is--," Little Dan turned to introduce Jerry.

Jimmy interrupted him. "That's Jerry Somerset. Everybody knows Jerry Somerset."

"Is that so?" Little Dan asked, looking to his deputy.

"Oh yeah. You shoulda heard my mom talk about you," Jimmy said to Jerry. "She loved Jerry Somerset. Apparently, she hired you to paint her house one year. You was just a boy, she'd say, but she said you worked awful hard."

"Diane Gibson your mother?" Jerry asked.

"That's right," Jimmy confirmed. "Anytime your name would come up, she'd tell everybody what a fine house painter you were. Said you even let her cook a big lunch for you every day. And you wouldn't leave the table until you finished every bite."

"That does sound like you, Jerry," Little Dan added.

"Your mom was a fine cook, for sure," Jerry said. "Made me soup beans and cornbread about every day, if I recall."

"The reason we're here, Jimmy," Little Dan began. But he froze as he looked at Jimmy on the porch and saw the young man was in a wheelchair and his right leg was gone, missing from above the knee.

"Yes?" Jimmy asked.

"I guess you've heard about Stanley Jennings, right?" Little Dan said.

"No. I don't hear much out here. What happened?"

Jerry stepped in. "Someone killed him on the night of the Fourth of July. We believe the person knew him and probably played for the Little League team he coached."

"Oh, that's awful. I did play for him, but that was before," Jimmy said as he rolled his chair around to them. "That was before I got in this chair."

The sheriff looked uncomfortably to Jerry.

"Y'all didn't know about this, did you?" Jimmy asked. "He wasn't run over with a wheelchair or beaten with some crutches, was he?"

"No," Jerry answered, smiling at Jimmy's good nature. "Nothing like that."

"Naw fellas, I aint got much for you, I'm afraid," Jimmy said. "They bring me my groceries and the UPS man comes up here to bring me these dulcimers, but I don't ever leave this holler."

Jimmy reached behind him and pulled out another dulcimer to show the two men.

"You collect them?" Little Dan asked.

"Oh no, I repair them. Or I find cheap ones online and buy and sell them. The UPS man brings them to me, and then he comes to get them when I need to ship one somewhere."

"Well, expert house painter Jerry Somerset," Little Dan said to Jerry. "Looks like we came out all this way for nothing."

"We got to hear some good music," answered Jerry. "So I wouldn't call it a bad trip."

"I guess that's right," Little Dan said. "Was mighty fine playing indeed."

"Thanks," Jimmy said to Little Dan. "But if you don't mind me asking, how do you know?"

"What do you mean?" Little Dan asked.

"You don't strike me as a dulcimer aficionado, Sheriff. No offense. So how would you know if I played well or not?"

Jerry beamed and looked to Little Dan for his answer. "Yeah, Sheriff. What exactly sounded good about what we heard?"

"What about Jerry?" Little Dan said, defensively. "He's not a music expert either. Why aint you asking him?"

"Jerry does strike me as someone who understands

good dulcimer music," Jimmy said. "You can see it's baked into him, in his bones. He can hear the rhythms and pitch of this instrument because it's the sound of the natural world. Jerry's a part of that world, you can tell."

Jerry let out a big laugh and clapped Little Dan on the back. "That's some of the most polite insulting I've ever heard. But he's got you dead to rights, Sheriff."

Little Dan felt cornered by the two men. "Well, maybe I aint as much a mountain man as Jerry, but I can judge a good dulcimer picker when I hear one. And you're a good one."

Jimmy smiled as Little Dan and Jerry began to leave.

"I got one for you, Jerry," Jimmy called to them as they rounded the corner of his cabin. "See what you think of this."

Little Dan walked on, but Jerry stood at the edge of the cabin, watching Jimmy strum his dulcimer. He picked out the gospel song *Farther Along* and began to sing.

"Tempted and tried we're oft made to wonder,
Why it should be thus all the day long.
While there are others living about us.
Never molested though in the wrong."

Jerry smiled to Jimmy and nodded his head as the strumming continued. He waved at the young man and turned to join Little Dan on the walk to their car. The dulcimer continued, and Jimmy sang on.

"When death has come and taken our loved ones.
It leaves our home so lonely and drear.
And then do we wonder why others prosper.
Living so wicked year after year."

Jerry reached the car and saw Little Dan inside, already crossing off Jimmy's name from their list. Jerry looked back toward the sound of the dulcimer and heard Jimmy one last time.

"Farther along we'll know all about it.
Farther along we'll understand why.
Cheer up my brother live in the sunshine.
We'll understand it all, by and by."

Jerry stepped into the car and asked, "So where next?"

Little Dan began backing out of the holler. "Next will be tomorrow." He found a wide spot and turned the car around. "That elk draw is in a couple hours, and I need to help Daddy get everything set up."

Jerry checked his watch. "Holy cow. I almost forgot. Too much on my mind, I guess."

"Yep, be careful not to stretch yourself too thin," Little Dan said. "You got a lot on your plate right now."

"When we get to the station, I'm going to run home and get my nephew to take with me to the draw," Jerry said. "Since I am over that way, I will check-in at the pawnshop and see if anybody has turned in Stanley's guns."

"That's a long shot," Little Dan said.

"It's never a bad idea to check in with Vernon though," said Jerry. "I sometimes think that guy is the one man in the county who knows where all the bodies are buried."

"Good idea. Check with him," Little Dan said. "Then I will see you at the draw. Maybe it's your year?"

Jerry nodded and tried to hide his excitement.

*　　　　　*　　　　　*

It's still over an hour until the drawing, you can rest here a minute," Susie said to Jerry. "You look exhausted."

"I'm gonna run by the pawnshop first. Got a few things to ask Vernon."

"Oh, about the big case?" Susie looked to Jerry eagerly, her big dimples forming as she smiled.

"Maybe," Jerry said, grinning. "I'm gonna take Andrew with me to the drawing."

"Oh, he will love going to an elk draw," Susie said, mocking her husband's plan.

Jerry's look back let her know he did not share her joking mood. "He seems like something's been bothering him."

Susie saw Jerry's demeanor change. She learned to recognize that helpless fear in her husband when he was up against an unworkable problem with his family.

"Does he seem like something's wrong?" Jerry asked her. "Maybe he's into something?"

"I swear I never know what's going on with that boy," said Susie. "It's untelling what he could have gotten into lately."

*   *   *

Jerry left Andrew in the car and walked into Smith's Pawnshop. Vernon, the owner, talked to a young woman across his counter. The two disagreed over the value of a sterling silver bracelet she offered to him. In his sixties, Vernon was tall and thick, solid like a man who had worked his entire life. His long, curly beard had gone gray decades earlier, but it still held a little auburn on his cheeks by his sideburns. Vernon's swollen arms were tattooed with vibrant designs that blended together in reds and blues. Indian and frontier artifacts decorated the wall behind his counter, next to framed "In Memorial" souvenirs of Dale Earnhardt.

"Can't give you more than thirty-five, sorry," said Vernon to the woman. Turning to Jerry, he said, "What do ya say, lawman? Be with you directly."

"But it's worth a hundred at least," protested the woman. "My granny said she paid one-fifty for it, ten years ago."

"Maybe it is, maybe it aint. But it's worth thirty-five to me. And how do I know you didn't steal it? See that feller there?" Vernon said, pointing to Jerry. "He might be here looking for you and this bracelet."

"No," replied the woman. "I've got a picture here of me wearing it when I was younger."

"Thirty-five is all I can do," said Vernon.

The woman looked to Jerry. He sympathized with her because he did not doubt the truth in what she claimed about the bracelet's value, but he could not offer her any support. She returned to Vernon with reluctance and nodded her head.

"Fill out this form and I'll see if I can talk my way out of going to jail," Vernon said, as he slid her a paper and a pen and turned to Jerry. "What about it, lawman? Whatever they said about me, it's a lie."

"Has anyone brought in any guns in the last couple days?" Jerry asked.

"Those guns again?" said Vernon. "That your kinfolk took from you?"

Jerry felt a sickness in his stomach, hearing Vernon mention his family's stolen items. His neck muscles betrayed him, as he glanced at Andrew in the car in the parking lot. Vernon saw Jerry identify the person who committed the crime just referenced.

"No, not those guns. This is a police matter," Jerry explained. "We're trying to locate--"

Vernon interrupted him, "I swear, any blood of mine that stole from me, well, you wouldn't have to worry about getting a call, I'll tell ya that. You boys down at the police house wouldn't even know about it. We'd take care of it ourselves."

Jerry put his head down, but he could not stop himself from looking out at Andrew again. He felt angry that he kept giving away what he knew Vernon suspected.

"Like I said, we're trying to locate a couple guns," Jerry said.

"So what is it you're looking for this time?"

"12-gauge pump Remington and a Winchester .30-06 with a scope," said Jerry.

Vernon wrote it down. "They were taken from someone?"

"Have you seen them or not?" Jerry asked.

"It's that killing the other day, aint it?" said Vernon. "Why else would you be stopping here on the way to the big elk draw?"

Jerry grinned.

"Yeah, I know where you're heading," said Vernon. "You aint got one of them elks yet, have you?"

Vernon pointed to the back of his store. A set of antlers arched above the door to his office.

"Yeah, yeah, yeah, everybody knows you got the best one last year," answered Jerry. "And no, I aint got one yet, but maybe this is my year."

"So if you are still playing Hardy Boys with the draw just a few minutes away, you must be working this big killing," Vernon said, proud of what he had just reasoned. "A case like this, for you, hell. Crack something like this would be good for your career, no doubt. Be the next sheriff for sure."

Jerry said nothing. Vernon saw he overstepped with those comments. He changed to a serious tone and said, "Naw, I aint seen them, lawman."

"Okay, if you do, give me a call," said Jerry.

Vernon shook his head in reflection. "Jerry Somerset, out hunting for the killer of Stanley Jennings. I swear."

Jerry paused and looked at the old man, seeing sincerity and tenderness in his face for the first time he could remember.

"If your daddy could see that," Vernon said, looking off. "That'd be something."

Jerry looked at Vernon and saw the man's thoughts return to a time long ago. "What do you mean?"

"Stanley was just a good old boy, Jerry. And your old man was too. He'd just been proud of you, that's all I'm saying."

"Thanks, Vernon."

"Absolutely," Vernon said and pulled himself out of his sentimental mood. "Now, go get this son of a bitch. Nothing I hate worse than a thief. Except maybe a murdering thief. I'll tell you what. If y'all down at that police house agree to look the other way, then whenever someone comes in with these guns, we won't have to worry about no arrest, no trial, no lifetime of hot meals. I'll take care of this feller for you. What do you say?"

"That's mighty generous of you, Vernon," said Jerry. "But I think we'll handle it ourselves."

"All right, lawman. I offered."

Jerry opened the door to leave. He heard Vernon say to the woman, "Hey sweetheart, you got them forms filled out? I got that thirty ready for you."

"Thirty?" she asked. "You said before it was thirty-five."

*   *   *

When Jerry and Andrew reached the park, a crowd had already formed in front of the stage for the elk draw. Jerry grinned to his nephew as they walked toward the people.

"This is exciting, huh?" he said to Andrew.

"Yeah, a barrel of monkeys," his nephew replied and rolled his eyes.

On the sidewalk, they passed a metal newspaper vending box for The Buckner County Times. Jerry paused and looked at the cover, a picture of Stanley next to the articles by Eddie and his son. Jerry pointed to the newspaper and asked, "You knew about this, right?"

"Yeah, Maw was telling me. It's dicked up," said Andrew.

"You played ball for him, right? Little League?"

"Yeah, but just for one year."

Andrew looked away, returning his attention to the crowd and the stage. Jerry studied his nephew, trying to get a read on his reaction.

"He was a good man, that's for sure," Jerry said.

"I guess."

As they joined the rest of the people, Jerry pulled out the tickets for the lottery draw. He handed three of them to Andrew.

"Here, you take yours, Betty's and Mom's," he said. "And I'll hold mine and Susie's."

"What does it matter?" said Andrew. "You bought them all and if anybody wins, you're gonna do it, so they're all yours anyway."

Jerry put his arm on his nephew's shoulders and pulled him closer. "Yeah, but it might be good luck if you hold them."

"I doubt it," said Andrew, pulling away from his uncle.

"I realized the other day that next year I can register the baby too," said Jerry. "That's six tickets for me. Another shot at winning."

"Register a baby to win an elk hunt?" said Andrew.

"Aint no law against it," Jerry said, beaming.

More citizens formed behind Jerry and Andrew, as the dignitaries assembled on the stage. Two vehicles drove through the lawn of the town center and parked beside the platform. The first vehicle was a green Ford pickup truck, driven by Steven Calhoun. Riding shotgun next to him was Big Dan. Behind them was an SUV covered in "Little Dan for State House" advertisements. Inside that vehicle was the sheriff, his wife and their two children.

Big Dan stepped out of Steven's pickup and raised his hands in the air. The crowd whooped with excitement. Little Dan followed his father onto the stage, as Steven and the rest of the Calhouns sat in folding chairs near a registration booth set up to process the winners.

The men on stage were dressed in suits and ties, except for Big Dan. He was fully outfitted in new camouflage, with a bright orange cap. He looked out at the crowd and asked, "Who's ready to go get some elk?"

Everyone cheered.

Big Dan took his seat and looked to the mayor to get the event started. The mayor approached a lectern and said into a microphone, "Okay everyone, let's get to it.

We're all here for the annual elk lottery draw. Before we get going, we want to once again thank Big Dan Calhoun for starting all this and donating the land that went to restoring these wonderful animals to the mountains."

The crowd applauded and Big Dan nodded.

"Forestry officials estimate the herds have tripled in size in these last fifteen years and now number over a thousand. The Department of Fish and Wildlife has given our county permission to harvest a dozen bull elk this year, and that's what we intend to do."

Big Dan pumped his fist, bringing a roar from the crowd.

"Twelve shots," Jerry said to Andrew. "Them's pretty good odds. We've never had that many before."

"If you knew how many people entered, I could do the probability for you," his nephew said. "You just divide by twelve and then again by five. Because you got five shots."

"I don't know how many entered," said Jerry. "But we'll know soon if we made it."

"We had two thousand entries," the Mayor said to the crowd.

"Oh, that's not very good odds then," said Andrew to Jerry. "Like thirty or forty to one."

The mayor continued, "At fifteen dollars a pop, that's over thirty thousand dollars that'll go directly back into restoring these wonderful animals to other counties. Eventually, through the work of folks like all of you, we'll have these mountains back to what they looked like when Daniel Boone first came through here all those years ago."

The crowd's thunder at that statement eclipsed everything before. It extended until Big Dan stood and waved to calm the people. Once the cheering ended, the mayor smiled and said, "So, let's get it started. The first tag goes to…"

He walked over to a lottery-style drum full of paper slips. He rolled it a few times and pretended to reach inside. But instead, to the delight of the crowd, he retrieved a slip from his pocket. He walked back to the microphone and said, "The first tag goes to Big Dan Calhoun."

Big Dan sprung from his chair and pumped his fist again. He walked to the microphone. The mayor stepped aside.

"I can't believe my luck," Big Dan said. "Year after year, first one drawn every time."

"You must be living right, Big Dan," said the mayor.

"I hear there's a big fourteen-pointer wandering around where Troublesome Creek heads toward the lake," said Big Dan. "All kinds of people seen him. I want everyone else to leave that one alone. He needs me to put him down."

The crowd groaned playfully, and Big Dan pretended to be surprised.

"What?" he said. "You won't leave him for me?"

"No way," someone called from the crowd.

"Well, I guess I will have to be out there early then," Big Dan said. "I'll just have to beat all you other fellers to him."

"Okay, thanks Big Dan, as always," said the mayor. He moved to resume his duties, but Big Dan stepped in front of him and retained control of the microphone.

"One more thing," said Big Dan. "When my oldest there was just a little feller in the fifth or sixth grade, he was learning about Kentucky state history in school."

Little Dan smiled and waved to the crowd.

Big Dan continued, "And his teacher was telling all them kids about how the white man came in uninvited to Indian land. She was saying 'the white man did this' and 'the white man did that' and 'the white man just plum destroyed everything' to all them kids."

Big Dan paused and looked to his son.

"So, Little Danny there, he had to do a project about one animal that used to be here in Kentucky but was now gone because of the white man. And he picked the elk. When he was doing his work, he came to me and said 'Daddy, if the elk was here at one time, why don't we just bring it back?' And I didn't have an answer for the little feller." Big Dan paused. He looked out over the group and smiled. "So, we brought it back."

The crowd cheered, and Big Dan continued, "It's as much owed to my son there as it is to me. And most of you know, he's now running for the State House of Representatives, and we'd appreciate your vote as we send him down there to Frankfort."

The mayor interrupted Big Dan and took back the microphone.

"Okay, okay, Big Dan, we aint gonna be politicking today," he said. "There's time for that later."

Big Dan returned to his seat and watched the mayor continue the draw. The crowd understood the next eleven names would be selected with integrity and watched the mayor pull winners from the lottery drum. With each name, Big Dan applauded and occasionally joked with the winner.

"Oh no, not Bobby Holiday," he said. "He's liable to drive a Sherman Tank into the hills and kill every darn elk he sees."

"You know it," Bobby said, as he retrieved his ticket.

After Big Dan and ten other names were called, the

mayor went to the drum one last time. He pulled a name and said, "And finally, the last tag goes to...Jerry Somerset."

Jerry smiled as the people around him gave congratulations and patted him on the back. He walked to the stage and retrieved his slip from the mayor.

"Go get you a good one, Jerry," the mayor said.

"I will. You know I will," Jerry answered. He held the ticket above his head, beaming with joy. He mimicked firing a rifle, earning laughter from townsfolk who were going away emptyhanded. Jerry returned to Andrew and smacked his nephew on the back, trying to get him to join in the celebration.

"We're gonna get an elk," Jerry said.

"You," Andrew corrected. "You are going to get an elk."

Big Dan approached Jerry and said, "Congratulations, Jerry. I'll be seeing you out there, I guess."

Jerry looked to his nephew and said, "Andrew, do you see someone standing here? I hear a voice, but I don't see anyone."

"Oh, because he's wearing camouflage. I get it," Andrew answered in deadpan.

Big Dan laughed.

"He could have played along a little, couldn't he?" Jerry asked Big Dan.

"These kids don't understand a good joke," Big Dan answered. The old man's tone changed, as he put an arm around Jerry and said, "Danny tells me he's got you on this murder case. Anything on that yet?"

"It's just a big old mess right now," Jerry answered. "We're looking at everything."

"I went to school with Stanley," said Big Dan. "Not

a finer man in these parts. So, whatever you need to do to catch that son of a bitch, you do it."

"I'll do my best," Jerry answered.

"Dad, let's go," Steven called to his father and motioned toward the green truck.

"That's all we can ask," said Big Dan. "The killer could be anywhere, so just keep looking for him."

Big Dan then joined Steven, and the two walked toward the pickup.

CHAPTER 6

I've had Andrew in my house just about all his life. Back when he was a baby, his mommy and daddy was living in a house that was plum awful. It had all kinds of dangerous things with the floors and the wiring, so me and Jerry went over there one day and got Andrew. Brought back diapers and toys, even this little swing I bought for him when he was born. He stayed with us for a few weeks until Betty got the place straightened up, and then she came back and got him.

But the second time he came to live with me, he stayed. Betty came with him that time, after she finally figured out that Andrew's daddy wasn't no good. And Andrew's been here just about all the time since. Well, that's not completely true. That one time, he did go and live with his daddy's people for about a year, and another time, a judge made him stay in a bad place for a couple months. He had to live with other boys who had gotten into trouble for much worse things than Andrew ever did. I don't know why the judge thought he should send him there.

But other than those times, my house has always been where he laid down his head at night.

I got custody of Andrew away from Betty that one time she went missing. That was after they came here to stay. Nobody heard from her for three days, and Andrew couldn't have been much older than five or six. I was having to tend to him and pretend like nothing was wrong, all while looking for her.

The police called us from Florida. She was with a bunch of people who'd gone down there. To get them drugs, you know. Them pain pills. They'd go around to all kinds of doctors down there and come home with a carload of them pills, a bunch of people all together. The police didn't have nothing on her, and she said she just went with them because she wanted to see Florida once. I don't know, cause that don't make no sense to me. She even told me she wouldn't have gone at all if I had taken her to Florida one time when she was little, like it was my fault.

Me and Jerry went down to get her, but we went straight to the lawyer the next day and Andrew has been mine ever since. She didn't even argue with me when we told her what we was doing. It looked like she'd been beat up or something down in Florida. Had bruises on her arms and a real bad eye. Jerry drove the whole way home, and Betty just sat in the back crying. When we got home, she went straight to the couch and slept for days.

I'm not sure what I did wrong with her. I guess I've not been the best mother, but somehow I raised Jerry too. That evens things out a little. Being Jerry Somerset's mom has meant I've heard, "You sure must be proud of him," all his life. And yes sir, I have been.

Some days, I will get ready to go to town and leave a few minutes early because I know I need to stop for gas. But when I get in the car, I see the tank's full. That's Jerry. I don't even know when he does it. He'll always make up an excuse, saying he needed to go get something for Susie and used my car, but I know he checks on it and fills it up when I'm low. Tires too. Brakes, everything. Things just stay fixed and maintained when he's around. And he never mentions it. Just does it and goes on. That's Jerry.

*   *   *

117

Jerry stood in the frozen food section of Adams' Grocery and checked items in his shopping buggy against a list he had on a notepad. Little Dan had a campaign event that morning and told Jerry he would be available to resume interviewing potential suspects in the afternoon. Jerry took that opportunity to complete another task.

In his cart, he had a loaf of white bread and a variety pack of sliced meats. The kind with real salami, not turkey salami. He had two large bags of chips, one plain and one barbeque. All that was left on his list was a half-gallon of old fashion vanilla ice cream. The cheap stuff with lots of fat and sugar. Not White Satin Vanilla or Creamy Dream Vanilla or anything other than just plain vanilla. "I don't want nothing all tarted up with them extra things you don't need," she'd say if he brought her something with a fancy name.

He pulled a plastic tub from the shelf and caught the breeze of icy air blowing out of the freezer, as he remembered that she liked to cover her ice cream with caramel. Bottles of syrup were on sale at half price. He snatched two and made his way to the register.

"Susie send you out to make a run?" the clerk asked.

Jerry smiled at her.

"How is she doing?" the clerk continued.

"Oh, she's having the time of her life."

"I bet."

The bill came to a little over eighteen dollars and Jerry paid with four five-dollar bills. He collected his bags and drove to Pump House Holler, the almost abandoned community that formed during the 1940s in a valley between Old Hickory and Big Water Mountains. At one time, thirty families lived in Pump House Holler, but a large part of Big Water Mountain began slipping in 2003. Emergency officials condemned every home in the holler, and the residents scattered. Whether or not the mountain slip was caused by a logging company, as well as how much the displaced families should be compensated, is still being argued in court today.

All that remained of the citizens of Pump House Holler were those who lived in a row of six trailers just off the main road. Jerry turned into that small trailer park and pulled into an empty parking space in front of the third unit. He saw the curtain bend on the large window in the middle of the trailer. He looked at the clock in his car and decided to wait five minutes before knocking on the door, giving her a chance to hide anything that needed to be hidden.

Jerry pretended to do paperwork in his car and check his computer. He looked toward the window again and saw the curtain pull back a second time. He saw her two eyes and dirty blonde hair. He got out of the car with the groceries and walked through the weeds and gravels to her trailer. She had no porch, only stacks of cinder blocks leading to the front door.

As Jerry stood on them and moved to knock on the door, it flew open.

"Jerry! I aint seen you in forever," Jennifer said and opened her arms to give him a full hug. Jerry stepped toward the entry and only partially accepted her embrace.

"You mind if I come in?"

"Mind? You know you're always welcome here, Jerry. I mean Deputy Somerset."

The combination of peach blossom air freshener and marijuana overwhelmed Jerry. He heard multiple fans running and saw the windows on the back side of the trailer were open, as Jennifer tried to remove a smell that had become a permanent character of her home.

Jennifer, thirty-one, was out of breath. Without pants, the Kansas City Royals t-shirt she wore barely hung below her underwear. When she turned, that shirt flipped up and Jerry saw the pink floral arrangement of her cotton panties.

"I brought you some groceries," Jerry said and walked toward her kitchen.

"Oh, you didn't have to do that," Jennifer said.

"I'll put them in here for you." Jerry stepped over a fallen broom in the floor of her kitchen.

Jennifer's face glistened, and she had a dirty ring of sweat on her neck. She pulled the front of her shirt up to wipe her brow and the bottom of the shirttail pulled up past her bellybutton, exposing her flat, empty stomach.

"I swear I'm a mess," Jennifer said. "Let me run in there and put something better on."

She skipped down the hallway and dashed into her bedroom. She shut the door, but it did not latch and partially swung back open. Jerry still saw her in the room. He watched her throw off her shirt and grab a towel to wipe off her face and neck. She turned back to the door and saw Jerry looking at her in only her underwear bottoms. He looked away as she slowly closed the door. She eyed him, seeing if he would look back before the door completely shut.

"I brought you some ice cream," Jerry shouted from the kitchen. "Do you want some now?"

"Oh my God, yeah!" she yelled back.

"It's vanilla."

The door opened and Jennifer's head darted into the hallway. "Just plain vanilla, right? None of that fancy shit?"

"Nope, nothing fancy," Jerry said. "Just plain vanilla."

Jennifer came down the hallway, now in a nylon tracksuit. She pulled her hair back into a ponytail. "Don't I look better now?"

"You sure do," Jerry said. Even with her pale, anemic skin and darkened eyes, Jerry only saw her beauty and recalled the incendiary combination of natural sex appeal and vibrant energy she had been when he met her years ago. The plumper, rosy Jennifer had been replaced with this sickly substitute, but being in her presence reminded Jerry of what had taken ahold of him when he was younger. He remembered the fun they had together on her couch as he watched her flop down on it and look to him.

"Did your wife kick you out?" she said, wiggling in her seat. "You looking for a place to shack up for a while, sailor?"

Jerry smiled as he scooped out the ice cream into a plastic bowl. "There's this case I'm working on," he said. "Thought you might know something about it."

"You here to accuse me of something?" asked Jennifer.

"No, no. Nothing like that. I seriously am running into roadblocks and hope you might have heard something. You know about Stanley Jennings, right?" Jerry asked.

"Yeah."

Jerry held the bottle of caramel for Jennifer to see. Her face lit up and she nodded. Jerry poured it liberally on top of her ice cream.

"What did you hear?" he asked.

"Just that y'all found him dead."

Jerry held the bowl in front of Jennifer. "Is that enough?" he asked.

"A little bit more."

"Nothing else?" Jerry asked.

"Like what?"

"Like anybody have any ideas about who it was?"

Jerry handed Jennifer the bowl and she immediately began eating, as he took a seat across from her.

"Nope. I just heard that they got all kinds of things. A laptop and guns. Jewelry too."

"They?" Jerry said.

"Whoever did it, you know."

Jerry watched Jennifer gobble down large spoonfuls of mostly caramel topping.

"Is that good?" he asked her.

"Oh my God, yes. Thank you."

"Who knows you like I do?" Jerry asked, and Jennifer smiled.

"Nobody."

"And who else brings you ice cream?"

Jennifer's smile faded and her voice dropped as she again said, "Nobody."

"So, what else have you heard?" Jerry asked.

"Is that really why you're here?"

"Yes, it is, actually. I told you."

"Not because you like me?" asked Jennifer.

"Well, that too," said Jerry.

"Then why are you all the way over there? Come sit with me." Jennifer patted the couch cushion next to her.

"I better stay over here. Less trouble on this side of the room."

"Uh-huh. I'm trouble?" Jennifer returned to eating and playfully teased by licking the spoon. "This is so good. Been so long since I had caramel."

"So, what else?" asked Jerry.

"Heard they was all kinds of pills up in there. They was saying he was eat up with cancer and they gave him a whole bunch of OxyContins. The big ones too." Jennifer set the bowl to the side. All the caramel was gone, but some ice cream remained. "You didn't use enough. I'm out."

"Want me to get some more?" Jerry asked.

"Naw, I will let it melt," said Jennifer. "I like to drink it that way, the ice cream when it melts."

"It wasn't no cancer," said Jerry. "It was knee surgery. No OCs either. Just Vicodin and Percocet tens."

"That's it?"

"That's it," Jerry confirmed. "But they was big bottles."

"Naw," said Jennifer. "I aint heard nothing."

"I didn't think you would, but it was worth trying."

Jennifer looked at him and saw defeat and conflict in his eyes. "You sure you don't wanna come over here? Aint it about time for The Price is Right to come on? We could watch it right here on the couch together, like we used to."

Jerry smiled and reached into his pocket. "I'm gonna be a daddy. Did you know?"

"You what?!" Jennifer exclaimed. "Lord have mercy. I never hear nothing."

"Yep. A couple weeks. Maybe days. Got a picture here and everything." Jerry took out the ultrasound and handed it to Jennifer.

When she took the picture from him, she reached past the photo and allowed her fingers to drag softly against Jerry's hand as she plucked the picture from him. He flinched and glanced up to see her eyes looking back at him. Those eyes, a mossy blend of hunter green and burned amber, then turned to focus on the ultrasound photo. Jerry saw a big smile form on her face.

It did not last. The more she looked down at the ghostly outline of the baby, the more she thought about how it would grow up in a happy home, with an engaged father. She was certain the future for Jerry's child would be one of wonder, and it would grow up lively and curious, excited to soak up all the world's magic.

Jennifer sighed as she handed the photo back to him. "Y'all know what it is?"

"It's a little girl."

"A little girl," Jennifer said, her voice trailing away. She sighed again. "She'll be a lucky girl to have you for a daddy, that's for sure. You'll do so much better than the other ones around here."

"I'll try," Jerry said, seeing a sullen shadow come over Jennifer.

"They come and took away my little guy, you know," she said.

"Yeah, I heard."

"They got him up with some family over in Letcher County. I get to see him every now and then. When I do, he cries. He needs his mommy."

Jerry said nothing. He pursed his lips and shook his head as if to nod that he understood. With a tear forming in her left eye, Jennifer looked to him and asked, "Is there anything you can do to get him home?"

"No," said Jerry. "There's not. I'm just a deputy sheriff. Would take somebody more important than me to help with that."

"I didn't think you'd be able to do much," said Jennifer.

"There's something you can do though."

"What?"

"You know 'what.' Get yourself straightened out," he replied.

Jennifer's eyes turned to the floor. "I can't do right without him. He helped me, having him here. Now he's gone, and it's too hard."

"He won't ever be back if you don't do better," Jerry told her.

"Aint right for them to just come and take him like that," Jennifer said.

Jerry did not reply. Jennifer glared at him when she saw he was not going to agree. "What, are you gonna argue with me?" she asked.

"No, but I'm not gonna agree with you either. Not about this. Look around. This aint no place for a little boy."

Jennifer scowled at Jerry. Without looking away from him, she reached for her bowl and sipped on the melted ice cream. He continued, "I aint saying that to be mean. Nothing I'd like more than to come here and see you two doing well. I know what he means to you, but wherever he is now, it's better than--"

Jennifer interrupted, "Get out!"

Jerry stood up. "I'm just saying--"

"Get out!" Jennifer interrupted again, screaming this time. She threw the bowl at Jerry and covered his shirt in the melted vanilla ice cream.

As Jerry stepped toward the door, Jennifer raced into the kitchen, threw open the cabinets and refrigerator and slung the groceries at Jerry. "Take this shit with you. I don't need your charity."

Jerry escaped out of the trailer, as the bags of chips and bread sailed toward the door. When he looked up, he saw a second police car parked next to his. Little Dan got out of the car and walked toward Jerry. He looked at the ice cream on Jerry's shirt and asked, "Lover's quarrel?"

Jennifer stepped out of the door, armed with a bottle of caramel, but when she saw Little Dan in front of her trailer, she ducked inside and slammed the door.

"What are you doing here?" Jerry asked Little Dan.

"I was coming back from that campaign thing and saw your car. I thought you were going to be doing research on court cases this morning?"

"Well, it's nothing official, but I do check with Jen from time to time on things, you know. She knows a lot about what's going on in the county," Jerry answered. "I thought she might have heard something about Stanley."

"Did she?"

"No."

"That's all you were doing here? Checking on Stanley?" Little Dan asked and offered a big smile.

"I'm happily married, Sheriff," Jerry replied. He did not return the smile or appreciate the implication.

"That's Jennifer Walker?" asked Little Dan. "She was a senior when I was a freshman. Lord have mercy back then, boy. Nobody ever wore a pair of jeans like that girl wore a pair of jeans in high school."

"Yeah, that's her. And back when I was single," Jerry paused and opted to keep the details to himself. "Well, back when I was single, things were different, you know."

"I know what you mean," the sheriff said, as he looked toward the trailer. "You had something with her

126

back when she was like twenty? Twenty-one?"

"Something like that," said Jerry.

The two saw Jennifer crack the door and look out at them.

Little Dan sighed a deep sigh. "She looked good back then, huh? I can only imagine."

Jerry thought about it and answered, "She looked better than she looks now."

*   *   *

"Don't reckon this guy is related to the old sheriff, do you?" Little Dan asked of Clyde Bowling, as the two men drove toward the address.

"The sheriff spelled his name with a double L," Jerry answered. "Clyde is a W-L. Pronounced the same, but that's two different Bowlings."

"Oh yeah, that's right," Little Dan said. "Those double-L Bollings were not from around here. Virginia, I believe."

Jerry and Little Dan drove the four miles from the police station to the trailer of Clyde Bowling. His home rested on a little hill about a hundred yards off the main road. A black dog chained in the backyard growled and lunged at their car, but the two men stayed away from its reach. Jerry stepped atop the cinder blocks in front of the trailer door and knocked. Clyde answered, shirtless and wearing jeans. He rubbed his messy hair and unkempt goatee as he looked down at the men.

"Ah God. What is it now?" complained Clyde.

"How ya doing, Clyde?" said Little Dan.

Clyde stepped out of the way and motioned for them to enter his trailer. Clothes, towels and pizza boxes littered the living room. On the couch sat Clyde's

eighteen-year-old girlfriend, Meredith. She held a
screaming toddler, trying to rock it.

"Clear out of here, woman," Clyde barked at her.
"Men need to talk."

"What do they want?" Meredith asked.

"Aint none of your business. I told you to get," said
Clyde, as he motioned toward the back of the trailer.

Meredith scooped up the screaming child and left
the room. Clyde smacked her backside on her way past
him. He smirked to Jerry and Little Dan, trying to gauge
if they were envious of what he just felt.

When Meredith disappeared into a back room, Clyde
said, "I saw you checking her out. Two old codgers like
you can't pull tail like that no more, can you?"

Jerry and Little Dan said nothing. Jerry crossed his
arms and glared.

"So, what did I do?" asked Clyde.

"What do you know about Stanley Jennings?" asked
Little Dan.

"Somebody blew him to hell," Clyde said. "If you
know who, thank him for me. I spent forty-three days
in juvie over that son of a bitch."

"When was this?" the sheriff asked.

"He called the law on me when I was fifteen," said
Clyde.

"For what?"

"Doing something behind that barbershop I
shouldn't have been."

"Maybe it was you killed him," suggested Jerry.

"Yeah, I'd think it was me too." Clyde paused and
pulled up his jeans to show an ankle bracelet. "But, if I
was the one did it, you'd already know."

Jerry gave Little Dan a look that let him know he
was sorry for missing that detail in his research.

"You have to stay home?" Little Dan asked.

Clyde nodded. He motioned toward the back of his trailer. "Not but one thing worth doing cooped up like this all the time. She's legal too if that's what you're wondering, and boy-oh-boy, what a wildcat."

"Yeah, nice girl," said Little Dan. "That your kid?"

"Hell no," said Clyde. "Had that one with her when I met her. I keep trying to get her to give it to its daddy's people, but she won't. I can't stand being around a noisy young'en, Lord have mercy. Sometimes it's all I can do to keep from throwing them both out that window yonder when they keep going on and on."

Jerry and Little Dan looked at each other. Clyde saw their discomfort and continued, "Aw hell boys, I don't mean that, but you know, they get on my nerves sometimes."

"Yeah, well Clyde," said the sheriff, "that's not good. Perhaps you should try being a bachelor for a while."

"See, I knew you had your eye on her," Clyde said.

Jerry steered the conversation back to the investigation. He asked Clyde for the specifics of his home confinement. He had gotten into trouble with the State Police in another county, and his profile had not been updated in the database. After examining the ankle bracelet and calling the tracking hotline service, Little Dan was comfortable Clyde was at his trailer the night of Stanley's death.

As Jerry and Little Dan began to leave, Clyde said, "Hell, stay around awhile, boys. Talk about some more crime. Unsolved mysteries, you know. Beats talking to that girl yonder."

"I don't know, Clyde," said Little Dan. "Do you have information on anyone you could tell us?"

"Well no, but I'd just like to hear what y'all are

working on," Clyde said. "I aint gonna rat on nobody, but maybe I could give you my expert opinion on something if it's one of them things I know about."

Little Dan looked at Jerry and shook his head no.

"Oh, come on," Clyde said. "That judge might take it easy on me if I tell him I helped y'all out on some things."

"I think we'll pass, Clyde. We gotta be going," said Little Dan.

Once they returned to the police car, Little Dan crossed off "Clyde Bowling" from his list, leaving two names.

"We need to call this into the social workers at the courthouse," said Jerry. "Somebody needs to come out here and have a visit with that girl."

"She's eighteen," said Little Dan.

"Yeah, he said."

"Well, she's an adult. Is she wants to spend her time shacking up with one of Buckner County's most eligible bachelors, that's her business."

"Still, with that baby. Somebody should just check on them," Jerry said.

Little Dan nodded. "I'll call over there tomorrow."

*　　　　　*　　　　　*

"I'm thinking we'll go over to Walker Branch Sunday after church," Jerry said to his nephew as they walked toward the backyard turkey lot. "We'll go right where Troublesome Creek forks. There's a spot I know where we can put up the tree stand. They have to be traveling that way for the water."

"Why do I need to go? I don't want to shoot no elk," said Andrew.

As their voices approached the run, the turkey poults ran to the side of their pen closest to the two men.

"Look at them running to us," Andrew exclaimed.

"Well, you won't be shooting an elk. I'll be shooting an elk," said Jerry.

"Okay, but I don't want to be there when you do it neither," said Andrew. "That's wrong, killing something on purpose."

"You at least need to go scouting with me and put up the tree stand," said Jerry. When Andrew shrugged and said nothing, Jerry added, "And Andrew, I aint asking."

The two watched the turkey poults flutter around the run. They flapped their featherless wings, chasing each other and pecking at the ground.

"Do you remember Jimmy Gibson?" Jerry asked Andrew.

"I guess," Andrew replied. "That guy without a leg?"

"Yeah, him. I saw him yesterday."

Andrew stepped over into the run. He looked to his uncle. "They've been out long enough. I bet they're getting cold. I'll put them back in their house."

Andrew began ushering the turkeys into their home. Inside, the poults collected under a heating light.

"He messes with dulcimers now," Jerry said. "Plays them real good."

"That's cool, I guess. I heard them things is hard to play."

Andrew had all the poults except one in the house. He pushed it toward the door, but the little turkey darted away from his hand and ran back to Andrew's feet, leaning its head against one of his shoes."

"That little feller thinks you're his mommy," Jerry said.

"He never wants to go inside when I try to put them up."

Jerry's tone changed, as he became more direct. "I was talking to Jimmy because of this Stanley Jennings killing."

Andrew sensed his uncle wanted to talk about something other than turkeys. He reached down and picked up the chirping poult and held it as Jerry continued.

"We're talking to the guys who used to play Little League for Stanley. Seeing if they know anything."

"You think Jimmy killed him?" Andrew asked.

"No," Jerry answered. He smiled at the little turkey chirping in Andrew's hand. "See? He does think you're his mommy."

Andrew set the turkey down and tried again to usher the bird into the house. "I'm not his mommy."

The poult darted again away from the house and ran to Andrew's feet.

"That little feller disagrees," Jerry said.

Jerry wanted to ask Andrew more about Stanley Jennings and the night he died, but instead he watched his nephew play with the turkey poult. Andrew ran to one side of the pen and back to the other. The little bird sprinted to Andrew each time, always wanting to stay near his feet. Andrew talked to it, while steering it all over the run. "Come on, little turkey," he said again and again, as the bird skipped to him.

CHAPTER 7

No, Jerry is not my son's daddy. Lots of people said that back when it happened, but his mom did everything she could to put an end to people thinking that. She made sure everyone knew he stopped seeing me a couple years before my son came along. And when Jerry cut it off, he cut it off for good.

I guess it don't really matter who my boy's daddy is, because the guys I was with during that time wouldn't have been like Jerry. I don't know how I thought it would work, but I kept thinking me and him would end up together after a while. I kept waiting for him to come back to me, kept waiting for him and that girl to break up for good. But they never did.

I could tell things changed with him once he saw me with a little boy. Like I was somehow damaged. Him and that girl that's his wife now, back when they was dating, you'd hear that they was fighting over something, maybe taking a break, and I'd run into him in town or send him a text. He was always polite, and he'd ask me about my son, but I never could get him interested in me. Not even just to come over and mess up the covers with me again. And I tried. I really tried.

He never thought what we was doing would go anywhere, I guess. I let myself believe he wanted it to, but he was just having a good time with me. I see that now. He never took me to meet his mom. She knew about us, for sure. I'd catch her glaring at me at the grocery store, and she'd drive by my trailer all the time. I'd ask him about that, and he wouldn't talk about her. When I'd say, "She must hate that you're over here with me," he would not argue about it.

His mom must love that girl he's got now, the one that's about to have his baby. She's from a good family, and she's never been arrested or nothing like that. I bet his mom thinks the world of her and they do all kinds of fun things together. You know, like they was mother and daughter.

*   *   *

Preacher Bryant stood in front of a packed congregation. The men before him mostly wore outdated suits and sat beside women in long dresses, even on this hot July Sunday. Most people held paper hand fans and kept small breezes going on their faces, trying to keep sweat from forming on their upper lips and foreheads, while they listened to Preacher Bryant's sermon from the Book of Romans.

The preacher looked out over dozens of swaying fans as he spoke of the Apostle Paul's three Es of Encouragement, Exhortation and Exaltation. Nearly all the fans he watched sweep and undulate had the same design on the front: an early 20th Century painting called *The Guardian*, by Austrian artist Hans Zatzka.

Zatzka's work, a favorite of Preacher Bryant's wife Nat, could always be found on stacks of fans in the church's foyer. The painting echoed the promise of God from Psalms that reads, "For He shall give His angels charge over thee, to keep thee in all thy ways."

Two children attempt to cross a perilous footbridge in the painting, above a dangerous, rocky creek. The children find comfort in each other, but they are unaware that an angel travels behind them, keeping watch over their journey.

The painting hung in the homes of many people in the church, but something about the angel depicted always made Preacher Bryant feel uneasy. Without context, someone might understand that the spirit guided the children toward danger, not away from it. Now the preacher saw more than thirty versions of that ambiguous figure flapping at him as he finished his sermon.

"I don't want to keep you much longer on such a hot morning," Preacher Bryant said. "But this week, we lost an important man in this little community. Mr. Jennings was not a member of this church, but I do remember seeing him out there more than a few times. I knew him to be a decent, God-fearing man, and anyone who knew him knows today he's wrapped in the Lord's warm embrace."

Dozens of calls of "Amen" interrupted Preacher Bryant's remarks. He paused and nodded in agreement before continuing, "I asked Brother Calhoun to sing for us this Sunday, a special song for Mr. Jennings."

Big Dan stood in the church's choir and made his way to Preacher Bryant's lectern. As the two men hugged, Jerry felt Mary's hand grip his arm. He looked over to his mother and heard her whisper, "Oh, Big Dan is going to sing."

Jerry thought he saw a little tear form in his mother's eye as she continued, "I love to hear that man sing."

Big Dan looked back at the choir, a dozen other men and women all solemn and serene. They waited for him to begin. After a cleansing breath, Big Dan's deep soothing, baritone voice delivered the opening line of *I'm Going To A City*. As is common in their church, the choir then sang the line back to Big Dan, pulling the tune to an unbearable, higher pitch and slowing their mournful voices to punish anyone in earshot. The twelve singers combined to form the harmonic equivalent of kerosene. As they gave the song back to Big Dan for his next line, Jerry heard the sniffles start in the pews behind him and looked to see his mother dissolving into tears. He patted her knee as she put her head on his shoulder.

When Big Dan finished the second line, the choir took over the song again to call the words back to him. Their voices lit the room with a sound that pierced the hearts of the most stoic churchgoers. Throats closed, chins quivered and little children looked to their parents with swollen, red faces. Big Dan's calm, gentle voice came back in alone for another line and allowed the congregation to gain control of their emotions momentarily, but when he gave the song back to the choir for their next turn, they melted the crowd again. The pattern continued through the life of the song until everyone in the church lay wrecked before the singers.

Jerry finished the song with his mother's head on one shoulder and his wife's on the other. He smiled to Susie and rubbed her hand, remembering that she should not get too emotional in her current state.

*   *   *

Jerry's cousins and aunts and uncles filled Mary's house, still in their church clothes. The children and women gathered in the living room, as all the adult men sat around the kitchen table, eating glazed ham, shucky beans and cornbread. Jerry did not speak of his investigation, but he talked extensively about the elk lottery and upcoming hunt.

"Me and Andrew is heading out later this evening to go scouting," he announced.

"Oh yeah, where?" his Uncle Oliver asked.

"Better not say. There's eleven other tags out there. I don't want everybody knowing where I'm gonna be."

Betty made occasional trips into the kitchen and asked her uncles and cousins if they needed plates or drinks refilled. On one stop, she saw that Andrew had slipped on his headphones and continued to eat. She walked behind him and smacked her son's head. "Take those off at the table."

As the men finished their plates, Mary and Betty collected their dishes and reset a place setting. Mary then called to the ladies to take their seats. Because of her condition, Susie was summoned first.

As she waddled into the room, Betty pulled the chair out for her. Susie looked up as she sat down and said, "Can't wait till this thing is out of me."

"That's cause you aint getting around, honey," Mary told her. "I walked up to Cleo's store twice a day when I was that way with mine. Never had no pain at all, and I had the biggest, happiest babies there ever was."

Mary retrieved a bowl of broccoli from her

microwave and put several spears on Susie's plate. "I made that just for you," she told Susie. "Need to eat something green every meal."

Susie shot a nasty look at Jerry, as he stood in the doorway to the kitchen. "She might not want broccoli, Mom," Jerry offered.

"Oh hush, Jerry," his mother answered. "What would you know about what a woman needs when she's like this?"

Susie continued to glare at Jerry, but he shrugged his shoulders in defeat and followed some of his uncles out to the front porch. He sat in a rocking chair next to his Uncle Thompson, just as the old man put in a plug of chewing tobacco.

After speaking more about the lottery and upcoming hunt, Jerry finally found the nerve to ask his uncle the question that brought him to the porch. "I was wondering if I could borrow your deer rifle for the elk hunt."

"You aint got you no deer rifle?" Uncle Thompson asked.

"Never needed one till now. This is the first year I got picked."

Thompson rocked in his chair, as he chewed tobacco. He motioned in toward the house and said, "Gerald had one. A nice one at that."

"Yes, he did," Jerry said of his father.

"Y'all never did find that stuff?" Uncle Thompson asked.

"No, it never showed up."

"And now you want me to loan you one of mine?"

Jerry thought about what was actually being asked in the question and crafted an answer in his mind. But before he said it, his uncle continued, "So I could end up seeing that one in there pawn it off?" Thompson stared toward Andrew through the porch window. While looking inside, the old man worked the ambeer in his mouth. He turned back to Jerry, locked eyes with him and spat into the yard.

"You don't have to worry about that," said Jerry. "I'll keep it over at my place."

"I sold all my hunting guns two years ago," said Uncle Thompson. "Just can't get back in the hills no more with my knees the way they are."

"I see," said Jerry. "Well, if you know anybody."

Uncle Thompson thought for a moment. "What do you think your daddy would have thought about all that? His only grandson stealing all his guns? And other stuff from your mom?"

"I don't know," answered Jerry. "I guess I don't spend time thinking about things like that. Too much else to do in life than sit around and think about the past that I can't change."

Uncle Thompson looked to Jerry and saw that any additional comments would not be met with polite answers. "I see," the old man said and spat one more time into the yard.

*   *   *

Jerry and Andrew walked along Troublesome Creek, searching for elk tracks leading to the water. "Look at this," Andrew called and jumped behind a fallen log.

He reached into the weeds and pulled out a three-foot-long elk antler. It was smooth like the bone handle of a pocketknife and had points longer than hammers. He squeezed his hand around one of the points, testing its girth. "These things is sharp," Andrew said to his

139

uncle and rubbed his finger along one of the tips. "Just about bringing the blood."

"Let me see that," Jerry said, reaching for the antler. After inspecting the base and points, Jerry announced, "Some folks would call this eight points, but these two here aint big enough."

"So, six then?" Andrew asked.

"Six," confirmed Jerry. He supported the scoring system that dictated a point must be at least one inch long to be counted, which disqualified two buds on the antler Andrew found.

"I'd like to find the other one," Andrew said. "I'd hang the set in my room."

"It'll be around here somewhere. They usually drop them pretty close to each other," Jerry said of bull elk's annual process of shedding and replacing their antlers.

While the two searched on the ground, Jerry looked above them on the hill and saw a large beech tree with a broken limb. The dangling branch made a natural arch over a large weed-covered boulder.

"Well, looky there," Jerry said. "Feller could put a little cover over that branch and use them limbs and weeds. Wouldn't even need a tree stand. Could just hunt out of that hole. You'd see this whole creek here and have a shot at whatever dropped this antler."

"If his other side is six points too, that'd give you twelve," Andrew said. "I thought you wanted a bigger one than that."

"He was twelve last year," Jerry said. "This is last year's antler. He's still carrying his rack this year. I bet he's sixteen or eighteen now."

As Jerry walked toward the beech tree, he heard an ATV engine approach. "That sounds like Big Dan again," Jerry said.

Big Dan and Steven came over the hill behind Jerry's beech tree, riding in Big Dan's buggy. After they stopped, Big Dan killed the engine and jumped out of his device.

"Jerry, I swear I'd just about say you was following me."

"Maybe I am," said Jerry. After a pause, he continued, "That was some mighty fine singing today."

"Well, thanks for that," Big Dan said. "I wanted to send old Stanley off right. I believe we did that."

Jerry nodded, as the two men met and shook hands.

"Dad, looks like they found the other one," Steven said when he saw Andrew's antler. He pulled its match from the back of their ATV. It was a mirror reflection of Andrew's antler. The two young men came together and held the antlers side-by-side.

"That's quite a pair," Jerry said, looking at Andrew and Steven and the antlers.

"Just like I told you," Big Dan said to Steven. "Sixteen points. Eight and eight. You gotta count them little nubs too. Aint that right, Jerry?"

Jerry hesitated. "Some people do count them."

"Did you hear that boys?" Big Dan said. "This here is a feller that don't cut corners. That's a sixteen pointer on my wall, but only a twelve on his. He's too honest to be a trophy hunter."

Jerry grinned a bashful grin.

"You thinking about hunting out of this spot?" Big Dan asked. "I bet you like that beech yonder for cover."

"I do. Unless somebody else has laid claim here."

"No, sir. You can have this hill if you want it," Big Dan said. "I hunted this spot myself two years ago and bagged a good one. I aint just ready to say for sure where I want to set up this year. Like to keep my options open. Man needs to have a lot of options."

Jerry looked over to Steven. "The way you drive that truck, I'd figure your dad would let you drive the ATV back this way."

"Huh?" Steven asked him.

"That's his polite way of letting you know to slow down on the road," Big Dan said to his son.

"When was I speeding?" Steven asked Jerry, without fear or worry.

Big Dan smacked Steven on the back of his head and said, "Boy, don't ever let me hear you question Jerry Somerset like that. I'm guessing Jerry here has had more than one chance to give you a ticket or else he wouldn't have said nothing. Again, this is his polite way of letting you know that."

Steven put his head down and said, "Yes sir."

"We're sending him off to the Navy, Jerry. Did you know?" Big Dan asked.

"No, I didn't. Danny didn't mention it to me." Jerry looked to Andrew and said, "I've been wanting to get this one here to do something like that too."

Andrew looked away from the conversation, as Jerry turned back to Big Dan. "How'd you convince him?"

"Oh, convinced hisself," Big Dan answered. "I just drove him down to the recruiter a couple days ago. Damn proud of him too. Young'ens here aint got much to look forward to, you know. Just always getting in trouble."

Jerry put his arm around Andrew and said, "See? Steven's got the whole world ahead of him. Getting out of here before it gets him. There's just a whole lot of nothing for young people like you too around here."

"Amen to that," Big Dan agreed.

Andrew said nothing.

Big Dan turned to Steven and said, "Why don't you give this young man your antler? They're only worth something as a set."

Steven hesitated, but he saw his father stare into his eyes in the way he looked when he did not want disagreement. Steven handed Andrew the second antler.

"Thanks," Andrew said and looked to Jerry beaming.

Andrew held the antlers out together, and Big Dan said, "You're right, Jerry. Them two do make quite a pair."

CHAPTER 8

After we dated for a while, Jerry took me with him into the mountains to gather maple sap. He told me I was the first person who knew where all his trees were tapped, and I figured that pretty much meant I'd hooked him.

"Now you can't tell anybody where all these are," he'd say of his sugar maples. And he meant it too. He tapped them trees all over the county, and none of that land is his. But he'd slip back in the mountains and put a tap on them trees while nobody was looking, and he'd say, "The people who own this land don't even know this tree is back here. They aint using the sap in it."

Every year I've known Jerry, he's hauled eighty gallons of maple sap out of the woods. That's enough to make two gallons of the best, purest syrup you've ever had. But you gotta cook it and cook it and

144

cook it to get it from eighty gallons to two. We spend the better part of two weeks cooking it down on the stove.

When me and him first started dating, he'd give the syrup to people in peanut butter jars or them old yellow and red mustard and ketchup bottles you see in restaurants. But I put an end to that. We only give the syrup to people now in eight-ounce mason jars. We make thirty-two of them and pass them out all over the county during the first week of spring.

I've even started buying them white screw caps to go on the top, and I ordered little maple leaf stickers to put on the fronts. When we get our thirty-two jars ready to give out, I tie plaid ribbons around the lids. They're as cute as a button.

We don't charge nothing for the syrup. Jerry said that's how he'll stay out of trouble for getting the sap off other people's property: by not making no money off it. He also makes sure all the people whose land he uses gets a jar of his syrup. That way he says they won't be mad if they ever find out.

That's the happiest I see him all year, those couple weeks toward the end of the winter when he's gathering all the sap and we are cooking it down to syrup together. During that time, our trailer smells like a stack of pancakes day and night.

That little kitchen in the trailer makes it hard to get it all done, but we make do with what we can. I'd love to have a big kitchen, even if it was just for the two weeks that we cook that syrup every year. I'd also be happy with a large enough fireplace that we could hang one of them cast iron pots on it and cook our syrup that way. That's how the Boones woulda done it way back then, and doing it like them would be something.

Yeah, Daniel and Rebecca Boone loved to make syrup together. I think that's what got Jerry started doing it. He loves telling people about the Boones and how they liked making syrup.

Every year I tell Jerry we should make one or two more gallons, so we will have more cups to give away. But he won't. He says it makes people appreciate it more because sometimes they get a cup and *sometimes they don't.*

"If you give the same thing to everyone, then you don't really give it to anyone," he'll say. I guess he's right, but I always want to make a little more every year when we're done.

*　　　　*　　　　*

Jerry and Little Dan walked through the tents and display tables of the Buckner County Outdoor Flea Market. Every Monday morning for the past two decades, the lot came alive with citizens selling ax handles, shotguns, clothes and homemade honey and jellies. The location was always a place for people to sell their secondhand items, as they shed children's toys or unwanted furniture. But in recent years, the market attracted permanent niche vendors, like the man who drove his van from Manchester every Monday just to sell wooden and plastic cooking utensils. He had an arrangement with an overseas factory and acquired his goods at a reduced rate. The man traveled all over Eastern Kentucky selling spatulas and ladles at weekly county flea markets.

As Jerry passed a covered tent, a voice inside called to him. "Hello, Jerry."

He turned to see Chessie, a sixty-year-old woman he always knew as a former acquaintance of his father. Not her real name, nearly everyone in the county forgot the full name found on her birth certificate. They referred to her instead only by the mononymous title she self-applied: Chessie.

"You set up here now?" Jerry asked her, as he watched her spin a kick wheel and etch with a potter's needle on a creation she would eventually work into a vase.

"Gotta pedal somewhere," she answered. Her tent was filled with ceramic pots, homemade soap and tie-dye shirts to match the one she wore. She covered her gray hair with a yellow bandana, folded and tied in the fashion common to bikers, although it made her look more like a clairvoyant than someone who rode a motorcycle.

Jerry did not know her when his father was alive, but he had several encounters with her in the two decades since. He had pieced together that Chessie dated his father before his parents began dating. More than once, Jerry wondered if Chessie's relationship with his father continued during his parents' marriage, although that did not appear to be a suspicion his mother shared. She loved Chessie's pottery and bought it both for her house and as gifts for birthdays and newlyweds.

Chessie let her wheel stop and stood from her workstation. After cleaning her hands, she approached Jerry and hugged him. As she pulled away, she let her right hand linger on his upper chest and collarbone. She patted and smoothed his shirt. "I swear, you always look so handsome in that uniform. It's like I was looking at your father."

"My dad never wore a uniform," Jerry laughed. "He always looked like he was two days away from being homeless."

"You didn't see him like I saw him," she answered.

Little Dan looked awkwardly at Jerry and stepped away from the tent, leaving the two alone.

With her high, sharp cheekbones and slender frame, Jerry never questioned what his dad saw in Chessie in their youths. In old pictures of her, he saw the lapis blue eyes and eternal smile that lingered in the woman in front of him. Chessie was always in the middle of those

147

photos, usually accompanied by insecure girls who did not welcome having their image captured while standing next to someone so full of life and beauty.

"You come to buy your mom one of my pots?" Chessie asked. "I dug that clay myself for the ones on the shelf. And it was real close to your all's holler where I got it. I bet she'd like to have one that came from clay around there."

"I don't know if she has room for any more of your stuff," Jerry answered. "She has them everywhere."

"There's always room for one more pot."

Jerry considered it, but money was tight. Susie would not approve of this purchase for Mary. Chessie never made Jerry feel pressure to buy things he did not want, but she did ask for his time occasionally. He received calls from her after her parents died and before the one time she bought a new car. Jerry always believed those were calls his father was supposed to take from her. He felt obligated to give her the comfort and advice his father would have provided.

The Letcher County jailer called Jerry one night and told him Chessie had asked for him. The Kentucky State Police brought her in for driving drunk, and she gave the processing clerk Jerry's name and number.

"You're going to Letcher County tonight?!" Susie demanded when Jerry told her he was driving to the neighboring county to get her out of jail. "Who is this woman again?"

"She was my dad's friend," Jerry said.

As he drove her home from the jail, Chessie turned and rested her head on his right arm before falling asleep. While she slept, she slid her hand down Jerry's arm and squeezed his pinky and ring finger. He drove the rest of the way with only his left hand, as he did not want to disturb her by pulling the other from her clutches.

At her home, Jerry admired the psychedelic tapestries Chessie used to decorate her walls. Inspired by the vivid, surreal floral designs she saw in her kaleidoscope as a child, Chessie blanketed her walls with a dreamlike exuberance. "I made them, you know. They're just big rugs," was the last thing Chessie said to him before disappearing into her bedroom and closing the door.

Jerry noticed a similar rug hanging in her tent. "Is that the one from your living room?" he asked.

"Good Lord, no. The one you saw in my house has an elephant in the middle."

"Oh yeah, that's right."

Jerry saw Little Dan looking at him anxiously. He motioned for the sheriff to rejoin them. As Little Dan stepped in the tent, Jerry asked Chessie, "Have you seen Benny Stone? We heard he sets up down here."

Chessie answered, "Yes, he's normally over by the dogs. I believe I saw him down there this morning."

"Let's head that way," Little Dan said.

As Jerry stepped toward the sheriff, Chessie grabbed him and hugged him again. "Bring your mom next week and buy her something."

"I might do that," Jerry said and pulled away from her.

Little Dan and Jerry walked toward the sound of the barking dogs, two Tennessee Coonhounds chained to the bumper of a rusty pickup truck. The men followed their barks and whines. As Jerry neared the end of the tents, he saw Benny behind his vendor's table. Benny saw the two men continue toward his display. He casually opened his money box, folded the bills and put them in his pocket.

"What's he doing?" Little Dan asked.

Jerry looked behind him to answer the sheriff. "Not sure."

When Jerry turned back, Benny was sprinting away from the flea market.

"Aw, damnit," Little Dan said.

Jerry raced after the young man and yelled, "Benny Stone? We just want to talk."

Behind the flea market was an open lot that backed into the forest. Benny cleared that lot like the all-state sprinter he had been in high school, jumped the ditch at the edge of the woods and disappeared into the trees. Jerry fell further behind Benny running in the lot, but he was confident the young man would tire in the wooded terrain. Jerry kept an even trot and looked ahead into the forest to decide which way Benny would run.

Little Dan followed, but only in a light jog. By the time Jerry reached the woods, Little Dan was fifty yards behind him. When he saw Jerry bound across the ditch and head into the trees, Little Dan slowed to a brisk walk and continued after them.

Jerry tracked Benny up the hill, following the path of disturbed limbs and seedlings. As he approached a clearing, he saw Benny's shoulder peeking out from the side of a tree. The body's heaves let Jerry know Benny had stopped to rest. Jerry looked back for Little Dan and did not see him. He crouched behind a tree and moved from cover to cover, closing in on Benny without the young man knowing he was near.

When Jerry was within a dozen yards of Benny's tree, he called to him. "Benny Stone? Just want to talk. What are you running from, son?"

Benny jackrabbited out from behind the tree and Jerry jetted after him. In Jerry's terrain, he closed on the young man, knowing how to avoid slowing vines and accurately judging which fallen logs would support his weight and which would collapse under it.

As Benny felt Jerry almost directly behind him, he decided to reason with the deputy. He turned to speak, but as he said Jerry's name, he saw the man's right shoulder spear into his stomach and next found himself flat on his back. Before he caught his breath, Benny was flipped on his face and handcuffed.

Jerry collapsed beside him and lay breathing in the wet leaves. "We're gonna rest here a minute," he said. "If you get up and try to run, I will crack your kneecap with my nightstick. As God as my witness, I'll do it. Just lay there and catch your breath."

"Yes sir," Benny said. He let Jerry rest.

After several minutes, Little Dan appeared and led Benny down the hill. Jerry followed and listened to the young man tell the sheriff how he went to a Cincinnati Reds baseball game on the Fourth of July.

"If you let me show you on my phone, I got pictures of me in the stands, and I got pictures of the fireworks they shot off after the game," Benny said.

"Why'd you run?" Jerry asked from behind.

"I thought y'all was after me because of them knockoff purses," Benny answered.

"What?" asked Little Dan.

"I'll show you when we get there," Benny said.

At his vending booth, Benny showed the two men a leather and soft suede hobo-style handbag affixed with a faux label for Coach.

"What do you charge for that?" Little Dan asked.

"Thirty."

"What's a real one like that cost?" asked Jerry.

"I don't know. Four or five hundred, I reckon," Benny answered.

Jerry looked at Little Dan. "What do you want to do?"

"I don't know," said Little Dan. "What do you think?"

"Now, hold on," Benny interrupted. "Aint this one of them things where you're picking on one feller for doing what everybody else does?"

"What do you mean?" Little Dan asked.

"Are you gonna arrest everybody?" Benny said, motioning his head toward the other vendors.

Jerry saw many other dealers watching them anxiously, waiting to see what they would do with Benny. Jerry stepped to the middle of the vending rows and announced, "Listen up, everyone. If you are selling black-market knockoffs of anything, pack up now and leave. This is your only warning. If you stay and you're selling counterfeit items, you're gonna be arrested."

The vendors all studied Jerry, but none of them reacted. Jerry returned to Benny and nodded to Little Dan. "Think we're gonna have to arrest him."

"Come on, man," Benny protested. "It's just fake junk for old ladies."

Jerry stepped behind the still handcuffed young man and walked him toward the parking lot.

"Woe now," Benny said. A big smile took over his face. He caught Jerry's eye and turned his head to the row of other vendors, directing Jerry to follow his lead. When Jerry looked back at the booths, he saw nearly every vendor filling their boxes and plastic totes with their wares.

"I swear," Jerry said. He looked back to see Benny

with his shoulders high and his chest proudly displayed. Benny reached his hands around to his hip closest to Jerry and jingled the handcuffs.

"You can go ahead and take these off now," the young man said.

Jerry looked to Little Dan. The sheriff nodded.

*   *   *

Little Dan crossed Benny's name off their list, as Jerry drove toward the address listed for Jack Ritchie.

"Daddy will be happy we didn't arrest him over them purses," Little Dan said.

"Why's that?"

"That's a federal charge. Woulda brought all kinds of people down here we don't want to deal with."

"Oh yeah," said Jerry. "Didn't think about that."

"And there are lots of Stones in this county. Lots of Stones, and they all vote. That's what Daddy woulda said. 'Lock one old boy up and cost yourself two dozen votes,' I can hear him say."

Little Dan felt Jerry's silence and knew it meant he did not believe either of those reasons rationalized their decision.

"Still, that boy was right," Jerry said. "That was enough for me. All he was doing was what everybody else was doing. Wouldn't have been fair to punish him and not everybody else there."

"That too," Little Dan said.

They arrived at the upper middle-class community where Jack Ritchie's grandparents resided. Near the hospital and largest elementary school, people built some of the nicest, modest homes in Buckner County in this area.

"We used to come up here Trick-or-Treating," Jerry said, as they neared their destination. "You'd get quite a haul from the people around here."

Jack's grandmother, Claudette, answered the door and whisked the two men to her back patio. After disappearing for a few minutes, she returned with a pitcher of sweet tea and two glasses for the men. She also carried a box of photo albums. After pouring drinks for her guests, the old woman flipped through the albums, looking for pictures and souvenirs of her favorite grandson, Jack.

Little Dan finished his glass of tea after a few large gulps and said, "That's the best tea I've had in a long time, Mrs. Ritchie."

"I aint afraid to use that sugar," Claudette said of her sun-cooked refreshment, so thick with sweetener it could almost be eaten with a fork. She refilled Little Dan's glass without being asked.

"Do you ever make it with maple syrup instead of sugar?" Jerry asked.

The old woman thought about it and said, "No. Is it good that way?"

"You can't do it like that every time, because it's a strong taste," Jerry answered. "But yeah, tea sweetened with maple syrup is a fine treat a few times per year. You gotta use that real syrup though."

"Oh, I never get the real stuff," she said. "It's too expensive."

Jerry made a mental note to bring the woman one of his cups the following spring.

Claudette found the album reserved for Jack. "Here it is. Let me show you. Now he's my third oldest grandchild, but just between us, he turned out the best."

Claudette flipped through the opening pages in the

album, showing Jack as a baby and going to kindergarten. During the middle section, Jerry saw one of the same Little League team pictures he viewed at the newspaper office. Near the end of the album, Claudette stopped at a picture of a young man putting aluminum siding on a building in a third world village.

"That's him there, building that school," she said. "He's already got into whatever law school he wants to attend, but he wanted to help build them schools for a year before he went."

"And he's there now?" Little Dan asked.

"Yes, he is. He'll be back in February."

"You must be awful proud," Jerry said.

"I am."

Claudette flipped back to the team picture in Jack's photo album. She put her finger on Stanley's face. "There's Stanley now," she said. "God bless his heart and soul. He was a good man."

The two men shook their heads in agreement.

"Now I don't want to tell you boys how to do your jobs," Claudette said. "But if you want my opinion."

"Please," said Little Dan.

"Yeah, go ahead," said Jerry.

"Well, if you want my opinion, you'll look at this little feller right here," Claudette said and slid her finger from Stanley to Andrew.

"And who is this?" asked Little Dan.

"That boy's name was Andrew Eldridge," she said. "He wasn't no count at all. His daddy would come to games half-drunk most of the time, if he was even there. I believe they caught that little feller stealing somebody's video game that year and he wasn't allowed to play no more."

Little Dan looked over at Jerry. Jerry did not look

back.

"Okay. We'll look into that," said Little Dan.

Later, as Jerry and Little Dan drove back to the police station, the sheriff asked, "Andrew Eldridge? I don't remember seeing--"

Jerry interrupted and said, "Yeah, that's my nephew, Andrew. He went by Eldridge back then."

"Okay?" Little Dan said, trying to understand why Jerry had not mentioned this before.

"I didn't have him on the list because he was with us that night, on the Fourth," said Jerry. "He went with Mom to the fireworks, and then we all came back to her house and we played rook."

"All night?" asked Little Dan.

"Well, till late," said Jerry. "When this happened, I thought he might be involved. But then I remembered that night and all of us at the fireworks together and then playing rook. It was late when me and Susie left. He was going to bed. It couldn't have been him."

As he drove, Jerry felt Little Dan's eyes on him, trying to get a read on the justice of his words.

"Yeah, but you should have said something," said Little Dan. "You went through those teams and didn't say anything about him. That makes you look like you're hiding something. Why?"

"I didn't 'not' say something. It just didn't come up," Jerry said and gave his boss a look to let him know the conversation was over.

*   *   *

Jerry left Little Dan at the police station and began toward home. As he pulled onto the main road, he slammed his fist on his steering wheel. And again, harder. Why not just be forthright about his suspicions on Andrew, he asked himself. What good would come of lying to the sheriff? He felt he had made everything worse by trying to make it better. Jerry slammed his fist on the steering wheel again and again. He pressed the accelerator to the floor and fishtailed into a curve.

As he squealed out of the turn on the other side, he saw a stalled car, partially in the road. The car's front end was mangled, with a busted windshield pointed toward Jerry. He locked his breaks and left a burnt rubber skid behind him, as he slid toward the stranded motorist. Jerry fought to keep his cruiser on the road and eventually came to rest a dozen yards from the car, with his right-side tires off the blacktop. After turning on his lights, Jerry rushed to the scene.

"Jesus, I thought you was gonna hit me," the young woman inside said.

"Are you okay?" Jerry asked.

When he saw the woman was uninjured, he pushed her car to the side of the road and returned to his unit to call in a report.

"What caused the accident?" dispatch asked.

"She says she hit a deer or an elk," Jerry answered.

"Is the animal in the road?"

"I've not seen it."

An EMT arrived and tended to the frantic woman. Jerry helped the tow truck driver load her car. As the wrecker pulled away, Jerry heard a long plaintiff wail coming from below the road, down by Troublesome Creek. Deputy Tackett had arrived at the scene, and he heard it too.

"Jesus, sounds like that creek is haunted," Tackett said of the mournful cry.

"That's her elk," Jerry said.

Jerry followed the sound of the whimpers. As he stepped over the guardrail and began down the hill toward the Troublesome, he picked up a trail of blood. The animal called again, the empty plea of confusion, pain and approaching death.

"Want me to go with you?" the nervous deputy called to Jerry.

"No, just keep an eye on the road."

Jerry neared the elk and heard the fluid-filled gasps and coughs of a dying animal. The spring-born calf saw Jerry and struggled to stand.

"Just lay right there," Jerry said. "It'll be okay. Where's your mamma, little guy?"

Jerry looked around but did not see any adult elk with the animal. The calf abandoned struggling to get away from Jerry by the time he was close enough to touch it. He saw at least one broken leg and blood too heavy for the animal to live much longer.

Protocol dictated Jerry should call the Department of Fish and Wildlife. Their local agent would want to visit the scene and decide what to do with the animal.

Jerry released a long sigh and tried to pat the elk's hindquarters, but the animal jolted and spasmed with his touch.

"I'm sorry, I'm sorry, little guy. You just relax right there and we'll get this over with."

"Want me to radio the Fish and Wildlife?" Tackett's faint voice called from the road.

Jerry stood and walked back toward the deputy until he saw the man looking down on him.

"Yeah, go ahead," Jerry called.

"And tell them what?"

"Tell them an elk calf got hit in the road and Jerry Somerset shot it."

"You shot it?"

"No. But I'm about to."

"You're not supposed to do that. You're supposed to wait for the agent."

Jerry continued to look at Tackett, but he said nothing.

"Okay, I'll call them," the deputy said.

Jerry walked back toward the elk, but he took a few steps away from the animal and approached the creek. He knelt on the creekbank and dipped his hand in the cool waters of the Troublesome. He rubbed the water over his dry face. He dipped his hand again and cooled the back of his neck and his temples with it.

In the cleansing waters of the Troublesome, a face looked back at Jerry. Lapping and chopping with the flow of the creek, the face knew the weight of his conflicts. As an omen of things ahead, the face in the water fractured and lost shape, becoming unrecognizable even by the man looking down on it now.

Jerry turned to the calf. Still breathing, but nearly motionless. He pulled his forty caliber Smith & Wesson pistol from his holster and approached the elk. Just as he leveled the sights on the calf, it turned its head to Jerry and let out one last wail.

*   *   *

Susie took dinnerplates from the dish drainer and stacked them in a cabinet. She saw Jerry at the table with a blank look on his face, as he gazed out the window to Mary's house.

"You okay?" she asked.

"Just a lot on my mind." He tried to smile at her.

"Well, your mom wouldn't hush until I agreed to let her take me to the store tomorrow," Susie said, reaching inside a ceramic cow on top of the refrigerator for money.

"You'll have a great time," Jerry said and allowed himself to forget about his day and instead focus on Susie.

"Forty dollars should be enough for what I want to get. She'll want to go somewhere and eat too while we're out," Susie said.

"You girls have fun."

Susie flipped through the bills from inside the cow several times, counting them. She looked at Jerry and said, "I thought we had eighty up here last week. There's only sixty."

Jerry looked back at her and did not say anything.

"It's the five-dollar bills that's gone. There were four of them. I remember counting this several times last week," Susie said. "You don't reckon he's been over here?"

"No," Jerry answered. "I took them."

"What for?"

"I had to get that stuff for mom's garbage disposal," Jerry explained.

"You sure? Seems like it was here after that."

"Mm-hmm," Jerry answered.

Susie picked the forks from the drainer and reached to open the silverware drawer to put them away, but the latch came off in her hand. A metal washer fell onto the floor, followed by the face frame and finally a fruit peeler that rolled out of the now unsecure box. Susie looked to Jerry in disgust.

"I'll fix this after you go to bed," he said. "Don't worry."

"We gotta get out of here," Susie said. "This place is falling apart."

Jerry conceded with a reluctant nod.

Outside, an SUV pulled in front of their trailer. Jerry looked out the window and said, "Well, that's Big Dan."

Jerry and Susie walked out to their porch, just as Big Dan stepped out of his SUV.

"Hope I aint bothering you, Susie," Big Dan said.

"No, we just finished supper. You want to come in?"

"I better not. I just stopped by to, umm, well…" Big Dan paused and walked toward the back of his SUV. "I know you already had that big party where all you ladies get together and play games and give baby gifts."

"Yes," Susie said and smiled at Big Dan's awkward delivery. "Shower was two weeks ago."

"Two weeks ago, right. I didn't get an invitation," Big Dan said and grinned. "But I was down in Lexington the other day and found myself at that baby store."

"Right," Susie said, giggling with anticipation. "You just happened to be in a baby store?"

"Uh-huh," Big Dan answered. "Anyway, did you get a stroller at that party?"

Susie contemplated her response. "Yes, I guess I got one." She looked at Jerry to explain.

"She don't like it. It's too small," Jerry said. He lowered his voice to a whisper and continued, "And it's kinda cheap."

"It would be okay to take it to the doctor and stuff," Susie said. "But I want to take her to King's Island and push her around all day. It won't work for that."

"I hope you got a receipt then," said Big Dan. "Because you might want to take that one back."

Big Dan opened the hatch on his SUV and pulled out a collapsible, canopied stroller, with swivel lock wheels, one-touch breaks and soft-but-firm cushions lining the inside.

Susie let out a little shriek.

Big Dan said, "I talked to a salesman at the store. That man said if you wanted to push around babies, this here is the Cadillac."

"That's the one I wanted," Susie said. "I saw it in a magazine."

Jerry looked to Big Dan and expressed his appreciation through a nod. Big Dan smiled at Jerry as Susie waddled down the porch steps and hugged him.

Susie pushed the stroller on the sidewalk in front of their porch. "It rides so smooth," she said.

"Can Jerry set that inside for you and let me borrow him for a little bit?" Big Dan asked Susie.

Susie looked to Jerry and saw her husband had not expected Big Dan's request. "Oh, I guess," she said.

"You sure you don't need him for about an hour?"

"I don't think so," Susie said.

"Mom's home," Jerry said to her. "If you need anything, she's right over there."

Jerry picked up the stroller and carried it into the trailer. Susie followed him inside.

"Where's he taking you? What does he want?"

"No idea."

Jerry looked to Susie and saw both fear and excitement in her eyes. He passed her on the way out of the trailer. She stood at the door and watched him go to Big Dan.

"Am I following you?" Jerry asked.

"No, get in and ride with me."

Susie watched her husband step into the SUV and

the two men drive away.

*　　　　　*　　　　　*

Big Dan said nothing as he drove, but he felt his passenger's nervous fidgets. Jerry leaned toward every potential sideroad they approached, expecting Big Dan to turn into them. Big Dan drove at a reduced speed and returned a wave to nearly everyone who passed him going the other way.

After they did not turn off on the road to Montgomery Creek, Jerry finally asked, "We going to the lake?"

"As a matter of fact, we are. But before we get there, I need to talk to you about something."

Jerry's mind raced. Had the sheriff told Big Dan about Andrew? Were they going to ask him to get off the case? Were they investigating Jerry for covering up for his nephew?

"Okay, what is it?" Jerry asked. He swallowed hard as the words left him.

"My boy's gonna win that election, Jerry. Aint no doubt about it. I aint gonna tell him or it'll give him the big head. But he's gonna win in a landslide."

"You sure?"

"Absolutely," said Big Dan. "If he was old enough, it wouldn't just be the statehouse I'd have for him. But he's got this one for sure."

"Even the other counties?"

"He's gonna hold his own in Letcher County and Knott County, but them other two boys are gonna split everything else there. Danny's gonna carry it here ninety to ninety-five percent. And we're the bigger county, Jerry. It's a done deal."

"I hope so," said Jerry. "He'll do a good job down there."

Big Dan smiled and finally looked to Jerry. He said, "But now, that'll leave an open job for us back here."

Jerry nodded.

Big Dan pulled off the main highway and onto a side road, leading to the lake. He continued, "Sheriff's an important job. An important job for an important man, Jerry."

They passed by the marina. Jerry saw several bass fishermen in boats trying to make a few more casts in the fading light. "We aint going fishing tonight, are we?"

"Nope, on up the hill."

The most coveted land in Buckner County spreads along a ridge overlooking the marina at the lake. Developed into Woodland Estates by Dr. Howard after he left the hospital, the retired physician has a bungalow on the hill and is often seen smoking a cigar in the evening as he watches the pontoons return to their docks.

The superintendent of schools lives in Woodland Estates, as does the mayor. Buckner County's one celebrity, a child star of Disney movies from the 1960s, retired to the largest home on the ridge. She rarely is seen in public.

Big Dan continued, "Sheriff's one of the most important people in the whole county, maybe the most important if you think about it."

Jerry sat frozen, afraid to speak because he did not want to derail Big Dan's words.

"Be a good fit for you?" Big Dan asked.

"Would what be?"

"Being sheriff," Big Dan said. "You're the best thing

that could have happened for Danny these years. He could always count on you; I could always count on you; and there's no doubt you'll do a fine job. I realized right quick that Danny wasn't ready for sheriff when we put him in. You woulda been right to be mad at me over--"

Jerry interrupted, "I don't know what you mean."

"Ah hush, Jerry. We all know it should have been you last time. I aint gonna make that mistake again. I got carried away and put my son into a job he couldn't handle. Everybody knows that. Just because he had the right last name didn't mean he was ready for the biggest job in Buckner County. But you've carried him all this time, and it's because of you that he's running now with an admirable record as sheriff. We owe it to you."

"I've tried to do my best," Jerry said. "For this county, and I didn't want to let you down."

"Sometimes this county is too much for a man, Jerry. There's so much wrong going on around here that a good, honest man often just gets chewed up. But not you."

"Shouldn't there be an election for sheriff?" asked Jerry.

"Yes, but that's what I'm asking," said Big Dan. "Do you want to win the election? After we set you up as interim sheriff, of course."

"Wow, that's a big offer."

"And I tell ya what, your election for sheriff won't be a close one neither. If that's what you want and that's what I want, you'll carry every district in Buckner County."

"I'll think about it if Danny wins his election though first."

"Oh, that's all taken care of," said Big Dan.

Big Dan pulled into the driveway of a darkened house. He jumped out of his vehicle and walked toward the front door. With caution and uncertainty, Jerry stepped out of the SUV and waited for instruction from Big Dan.

"There's a gun in the back there, Jerry. Why don't you bring her inside?"

Jerry opened the hatch of the SUV. Inside, a rifle was wrapped in an Appalachian quilt, the checkerboard design. Solid white squares alternated with dark blue blocks adorned with dogwood blooms. Jerry did not unwrap the quilt, but carried the full bundle inside the house, after Big Dan.

Big Dan walked around the empty house, turning on lights. He opened the refrigerator and took out two bottles of beer and put them on the kitchen bar. He looked to Jerry and said, "Put her down there."

Jerry carefully put the quilt bundle on the kitchen bar, away from the two bottles. He looked to Big Dan.

"I've heard you're short on artillery for the big day, Jerry. Open her up."

Jerry pulled open the quilt. Wrapped inside was a Beretta 501 bolt-action rifle. Jerry picked it up, astonished. He pulled it close to him, examining the craftsmanship of the stock and barrel.

"A Beretta," he said, breathless.

"That's the 501-sniper rifle, Jerry. Made by what can only be called 'artisans' over there in Italy. Hand-carved wood, with just a subtle varnish to pull out the grain, engravings, etchings in the metal, precise calibration. Every action is smooth and true. Pull that bolt and see."

"A Beretta," Jerry said again, as he pulled the bolt toward him and looked inside the chamber. "A Beretta."

"Yes, a Beretta," Big Dan said and laughed. He put his arm around Jerry. "That company goes back to the 1500s, and the rifle you're holding came from their main factory over there.

"In Brescia?" Jerry asked.

"That's right. You know your rifles. There's a few phony factories popping up all over the world, where they make guns and put the Beretta name on it. Like there's one in Tennessee. What would anyone in Tennessee know about excellence?"

Jerry laughed.

"But you're now holding one from the Brescia factory. The real Beretta factory in Italy. I've toured that factory. My grandmother on my mom's side was Italian. Did you know that?"

"No, I didn't," Jerry said.

"Yep, quarter Italian. Nonna came over with her father. She made us call her 'Nonna.' They came through Ellis Island, all that. I've been drawn to that part of my background because I loved my Nonna, and when I heard the best damn snipers in the desert fighting Saddam's boys were Italian fellers shooting these things, I knew I had to have one."

"Jesus," Jerry said, shaking his head. "A Beretta."

"You gotta stop saying that. I wish I had some shells; we'd go shoot something right now. You know, she's never been fired."

"Never?"

"Well, they probably shot her once or twice at the factory, but I've not shot her."

"I've never even seen a Beretta sniper rifle, and I've seen a lot of guns," Jerry said. "I didn't think these things even left the country, because they're only used by Italian military and police over there."

Big Dan grinned and said, "Well, you gotta know somebody. She cost me a pretty penny, so this is just a loan for hunting season, okay?"

"Yeah, no doubt. I'll certainly take care of it," said Jerry.

"I know you will. Bag you a big one, and then give her back to me. Man would get lonesome if he went without a beauty like that for too long."

Jerry placed the rifle back down in the dogwood blanket. The slight thump on the bar echoed through the house's empty walls and bare hardwood floors.

"Whose house is this anyway?" Jerry said. "It's just empty?"

"It's mine, Jerry. That's the real reason we're here."

"Oh yeah? Trying to sell me a house?" said Jerry, laughing at the thought of affording such a place.

"Something like that," said Big Dan. "I had this place built when I split up with my first wife. Had to stick her someplace or she was going to take my real house. I couldn't let her have Casa de Calhoun."

"You built this house for her?" asked Jerry.

Big Dan looked around and smiled. "Pretty nice, aint it?"

"Good going away present for a marriage, I'd say."

"She seemed to like it and was happy here the rest of her days. We wasn't together, but it made me happy knowing she liked it here. It's been empty ever since she's been gone."

"Dan, I aint in a position to--" Jerry began.

Big Dan interrupted and said, "What I was thinking was; well, you're about to be a daddy. And you're about to be sheriff--"

"I didn't say--" Jerry tried to cut in, but Big Dan did not let him finish.

"I said you're about to be sheriff. And you live in a little trailer next to your mom. Now I appreciate wanting to be near your people, but it's time for you to live your own life, Jerry Somerset, and become a serious man."

"But like I was saying--" Jerry tried to jump in again.

Big Dan interrupted and said, "Now, I aint looking to sell my house. Not with the market the way it is. But I figure you could move in and take care of it for me."

"For nothing?"

"Well, we'll figure out something for payment," said Big Dan. "The IRS would see to that. You can stay here ten or twelve years, and throw me a little rent here and there if you can. Make sure you keep it up, be good to your neighbors, you know. Get your family started. Save money. By then, I might be ready to sell."

"A little rent, here and there?" said Jerry.

"Sure, when you can," said Big Dan. "If you can't afford nothing for a spell, that's fine too."

Jerry shook his head. He studied Big Dan's cheerful expression. Jerry took a deep breath and asked the one question he had thought about his entire life. "How much are you worth?"

Big Dan let out a big laugh. "I have no idea. I used to pay Jason Harper to count it for me, but with what he charged and what he skimmed, I eventually figured it was better just not knowing. That way I'd have more anyway."

"I don't know what to say, Big Dan."

"How about start by saying this: I. Will. Be. Your. Sheriff."

"Absolutely," said Jerry. "I'll be your sheriff."

Big Dan shook Jerry's hand. "Let's have a drink, Jerry. A toast." He grabbed the two beers, twisted one open and handed it to Jerry.

"A toast? To what exactly?"

"The future, Jerry. The future."

CHAPTER 9

We've not had a little girl in our family in over forty years. That don't seem possible, but it's true. The last time I held one that was mine, I was about Andrew's age, and that don't seem possible neither.

Yeah, we've had Andrew come along in the meantime, but holding a little boy and holding a little girl aint the same. With little girls, you get to put all them little frilly things on them and dress them up like they was baby dolls. You can't do that with little boys.

Jerry's Susie don't know it, but when her girl comes along, its mamaw is going to have a house full of pink stuff for her to wear. A little girl wants to look like a little girl, so I've been getting things here and there and putting them away for it. All those things will stay at her mamaw's house, and when she comes over here, me and her will play dress up.

It's untelling how many little hairbows and ribbons I've bought for her. I just can't stop buying them, whenever I see them anywhere. I'm getting the two kinds, both the ones you use if she has a head of hair and those for when you have to cheat and just wrap around its whole head.

I sure don't want her to be baldheaded though. Her aunt Betty was baldheaded, and I felt awful taking her out in public. I put them little bonnets on her, because I didn't want to see people looking at my little baldheaded baby. Jerry's Susie has a nice head of hair, and Jerry does too. I'm praying that means their little one can wear the real hairbows when she gets here.

I'm excited to hold it as a baby, but I also look forward to having my little granddaughter right next to me as she grows up. I think about standing here on my porch and seeing a little one skip across the yard to come to her mamaw's house.

When I think about that, I always imagine her coming to my house in an ugly outfit, because Jerry's Susie is buying some of the worst things for a little girl you've ever seen. But then once she gets to her mamaw's house, she'll dress into something like a little girl will want to wear. Over here, she'll be a princess.

*   *   *

Jerry sat at the kitchen table of their trailer, eating bacon and pancakes and drinking an Ale-8 with his breakfast. Only midway through July, that morning he finished the last of the maple syrup he and Susie cooked in the spring.

"It'll have to be from the store the rest of the year, I reckon," he said.

"I don't know why you just don't make more," Susie said. "Or not give as much away."

"Those first pancakes with the real syrup next spring will taste so much better after I've had to choke down the fake stuff though."

Susie dropped it. She wanted to hear more about the house Jerry toured the night before. "How many bedrooms was it?" she asked.

"I counted four," said Jerry, "but I got turned around in there and aint sure what all it's got."

"And a big kitchen?"

"The kitchen and dining room is probably bigger than this whole trailer," said Jerry.

"Can't imagine what it's like," she said. "I bet it's got a big, beautiful stove."

"Stoves," Jerry said. "More than one."

"There's two stoves in the kitchen?"

"Not in the kitchen. But there's this parlor with the biggest fireplace you've ever seen. The fireplace has a little cookstove built into the side of it, and it's got racks and hooks inside where the fire is too. So, you can cook in there if you want."

"You can hang Dutch ovens and pots in there?"

"You could hang one in there in two minutes," Jerry said calmly. "It's already set up for you."

"You don't seem excited," said Susie.

"It just feels like we'd owe him," said Jerry. "You don't wanna owe Big Dan."

"Owe? He's not worried about money. He's got more money than--"

Jerry cut her off. "It's not money that we'd owe him."

"What then?"

"Loyalty."

"You just don't want to move away from your mom and them," said Susie. "You're gonna let them hold you back all your life."

"Well, it is all the way across the county," said Jerry. "And when weather's bad, Mom would be stuck over here."

"I knew it."

"And there's him too. I just don't feel like I should

move away from him, and I know you wouldn't let him come with us."

"Jerry, that's not your boy to raise." Susie walked over to Jerry and sat on his leg. She took his hand and put it on her stomach. "This is your child, Jerry. Andrew's grown up. It's time for him to live his own life, and you need to get on to us and our family."

"There's something else."

"What?" asked Susie.

"He wants me to be sheriff if Little Dan wins the election." Jerry tried not to smile, but when his eyes met Susie's, his face betrayed him.

"Sheriff? See? Everyone knows you're perfect for the job and it's long overdue. But doesn't there have to be an election?"

"He said not to worry about it," said Jerry. "Said I'd win if he backed me."

"I guess he'd know," Susie replied. "I'm gonna be married to the sheriff of the whole county. And live with him in a big house with four bedrooms and two stoves, one in a parlor."

"That parlor had a pool table too. I used to love to play," said Jerry.

"A pool table?"

"Yep."

"I guess I could let you keep a pool table," said Susie.

"This is pretty good, huh?" Jerry said, trying to absorb some of Susie's joy.

"Good? This is great," said Susie. "But I've known it since I met you. I've always known something good was going to happen for you. I knew it was just a matter of time before that paid off for you. For us."

*   *   *

Jerry stood in front of his dry erase board. He took a picture of all the notes he had next to the names before he erased the reasons why each boy was dismissed as suspects. He wiped the board clean until all that remained were the original names. Jerry wrote "Andrew Eldridge, aka Andrew Somerset" at the bottom of the list. He stepped back and looked at the name.

Little Dan entered the room. He saw Jerry looking at the list. "What now? Start over?" Little Dan said. "See if we missed something?"

"We could do that," said Jerry. "Or maybe that thing on the wall didn't mean what we think. You consider that?"

As Little Dan pondered the question, the phone in the office rang.

Jerry answered it on speaker.

"A Jennifer Walker for you, Jerry."

"Another ice cream party?" Little Dan teased.

"Did she say what she wants?" Jerry asked.

"She just said she had something for you."

"I'm sure she does," said Little Dan.

Jerry glared at him. "Okay, put it through."

*   *   *

"Aint gonna be throwing no ice cream, are ya?" Jerry asked. He stood in Jennifer's trailer, which was noticeably neater than his last visit. Strewn clothes and food wrappers that had littered the corners of her home were gone. Bowls of fresh potpourri sweetened the air around the end tables in her living room, and a copy of the Bible lay beside her recliner.

"I'm so sorry about that," she said. Jennifer moved livelier than before, and in just a few days, her cheeks appeared to swell with life. They looked like how Jerry remembered them when he would stop at her trailer years ago to watch The Price is Right. Jennifer even spoke faster and was in more control of her thoughts and words. "It was so sweet of you to bring me ice cream, and I paid you back by throwing it at you. I'm so dumb, I swear. The only person in this whole wide world who cares about me and I throw ice cream at him."

"How are ya?" asked Jerry. "You seem good. Better."

Jennifer moved to hug him, but Jerry kept it at a friendly, shoulder hug.

"I'm great. How is your wife? And your baby? How is it coming along?"

"Any day now," said Jerry. "They say ten days or so, but I think she's ready to pop."

"If she needs anything, you let me know," said Jennifer. "I'm serious too. I went through one myself and I didn't have nobody to tell me nothing."

"I'll sure tell her," Jerry said and waited for Jennifer to explain the call.

"Okay, I was thinking about what you said. About how I needed to do better, you know."

"Yeah."

"And a big part of that is being honest," said Jennifer, "especially with people who care about me. Like you."

"Good. That's good," said Jerry.

"I got to thinking about what you was asking about that man that got killed and those pills they took from him," said Jennifer.

"Yeah?"

"I remembered last week, after it all happened, running into this guy at a party who was trying awful hard to get me on some Percocets. I was telling him that they hurt my stomach. But he said he had a whole pile of them and was willing to let them go for awful cheap."

"Tell me about him," said Jerry.

"Well, first I really don't think he was wanting any money for them. I just think he liked me, you know?"

"You probably know how to read guys," Jerry agreed. "What was he like?"

"He was younger. Way too young for me. He wore his hair like them kids out in California, with it over in his eyes."

"Anything else?" asked Jerry. "Size, weight?"

"He was average, I guess. But skinny. Oh. And he wore a little toboggan. I swear he looked like them people you see on TV. What do they call them, goth people?"

"Did you ever see him again or exchange numbers or anything?" asked Jerry.

"Naw," said Jennifer. "He was trying real hard, you know. To get me. But he's a kid. I aint got no use for somebody like that. More trouble than they worth. But he was trying. Because I look good, huh?"

Jerry forced an uncomfortable smile. He turned his back to Jennifer and took out a picture from his wallet of him with Andrew. He placed his thumb over himself in the picture and turned to show it to her.

"Is this the boy?" he asked. Jerry steadied the picture with the thumb and index finger of his second hand because the one that held the picture trembled. He told himself it was because of the awkward way he had his thumb extended. He watched Jennifer scan the picture before she turned those mossy green eyes toward him, the same eyes into which he used to look and dream and escape and forget. Waiting for her answer, he felt scared in a way he did not understand.

"Yeah, that's him," she said. "Who's that?"

"He's just a guy we're looking at," Jerry replied. He struggled to swallow and stepped back toward the door. "Is that it? Anything else you remember about him and that night?"

"That's it," she said.

Jerry put the picture away and turned to the door to leave.

"You can't stay around a while?" Jennifer asked. She stood before him with a hand on one hip and some pout in her lips. She looked to the couch. "Price is Right is about to come on."

Jerry forced another smile and continued to the door. Jennifer dashed to meet him there and threw her arms around him before he stepped out of the trailer. She felt his discomfort.

"I don't care. I'm giving you a real hug, whether you want one or not. Why can't everybody treat me like you?" she asked.

"Treat people well, and they'll be nice to you back," Jerry said. "You'll see."

Jennifer moved to kiss him, and Jerry turned his cheek to meet her lips.

*   *   *

Jerry sat alone at his desk at the police station, typing out an investigation form. In the report, he detailed the conversation he had with Jennifer. He named Andrew as a suspect in the murder of Stanley Jennings and recommended the case be taken over by the State Police because of his conflict of interest. Once he was comfortable with what was written, he put the report in an interoffice mail enveloped marked "confidential" and walked to the break room, where he slid it into the sheriff's mailbox.

Jerry walked out of the empty break room, but when he got into the hallway, he darted back into the room and retrieved the envelope. He took it back to his desk, where he wadded it into a ball and threw it into his trash can.

He escaped to the investigation room, where he turned off the lights, sat at the desk and cried. His face turned hot and red, and his cheek touched the cold surface of the desk. It felt so good, he let it stay. He rested his head on the cold desk in the quiet, dark room long enough to fall asleep.

When he woke, he went back to his desk. He saw the wadded report in the trash. He took it out, went to the restroom and flushed it in pieces down the toilet.

"Aw God," Jerry said, as he saw the mess of a man looking back at him in the bathroom's mirror. He decided that man should not rush into a decision. Andrew deserved a chance to tell his story.

*   *   *

"What are you doing home at this time?" Susie asked Jerry as he entered their trailer. She was reclined in her favorite chair in the living room, with a fan blowing on her.

"Was just in the area and thought I'd check in on you. How do you feel?"

"I'm real hot," she said. "I've got the air up as high as it will go."

Jerry put his hand on her forehead. "Do you want me to get you anything?"

Susie patted his leg and smiled. "No, I'm good."

Jerry stepped out the back door of the trailer and walked into the overgrown weeds beyond their backyard. He passed through waist-high bulrush in the swampy ground as he approached Troublesome Creek. At the creek's edge, he mucked through cattails and scrub willows until he arrived at the large, flattop boulder that he and Andrew would use as both a picnic area and place to store tackle when fishing the Troublesome.

On that rock, Jerry taught Andrew how to catch small creek chubs with a fly rod and use those chubs as bait for the lunkers deep in the creek's pools. He saw some of those chubs darting in the water below him, and he thought about Andrew atop that rock, learning the rhythm of fly casting.

The first chub little Andrew ever pulled from the creek was no bigger than his pinky finger, but it made the perfect size to lure a cranky rock bass or smallmouth from under a protective overhanging branch.

"That's a good one," Jerry said to eight-year-old Andrew.

Andrew took the thin minnow in his hands and tried to get a hook in its back.

"I can't get it," said Andrew. "He won't be still."

As Andrew pressed the hook into the scales, the chub squirmed out of his hand. It landed on the rock, flopped once and bounced back into the Troublesome. Little Andrew rushed to the edge of the rock to watch it swim away.

"Wait!" called Andrew. "Come back."

"You was at one fish for a minute or two, but now you're back to zero. Let me do one for you," said Jerry. He slung the fly lure and dropped it softly above a school of chubs. One accepted Jerry's invitation and he flipped it out of the water in an instant.

"That was so fast," Andrew said.

"You'll get there," said Jerry.

Jerry picked up the reel cast pole and speared the minnow on the hook.

"It's ready for you now," Jerry said to his nephew. "Cast right over there in that dark water."

"Under that tree?"

"You got it. That's where the big ones live."

Later in the day of Andrew's first fishing trip on the Troublesome, he and Jerry walked up the path from the creek to Mary's backyard. Jerry lugged all the tackle and picnic supplies, while little Andrew only carried one item: a bucket that was a temporary home to a nine-inch smallmouth bass swimming in a few inches of water.

"Your mamaw is going to be so proud when she sees that," said Jerry. "I bet she cooks it for you right now."

The bucket was heavy for the boy, and he had to stop a few times to switch it from one hand to the other.

"Want me to carry it for you?" Jerry asked.

"No, I want to take it the whole way."

Jerry walked that same path today, this time alone. When he neared Mary's house, the memory of the happy day with Andrew from long ago faded. He saw the young man in the backyard with his grandmother and knew it was time to confront him about what he did the night of Stanley's death.

Mary saw Jerry step out of the bulrush and enter her backyard. She called to him, "You wanna get your hands dirty?"

Jerry saw that his mother and Andrew were working in one of her flowerbeds. "Y'all seem to be doing just fine."

Jerry stepped on the back porch and sat in Mary's swing. He watched Andrew with the posthole diggers, making a place for Mary to plant a small shrub.

"What is this one now, Mamaw?" Andrew asked Mary.

"An azalea."

"What's it like?"

"They're cousins to rhododendrons," Mary explained. "Like out front. Bloom like them too, with a dark flower. The radio said these is good for hummingbirds. I want to bring them back like they was when your papaw was alive."

"You could just get those bottles," said Andrew. "With that red stuff in it."

"Your pap never liked those. He always said that was cheating, using them bottles. He liked to give them hummingbirds flowers instead. There was a time when this whole bed was nothing but daffodils," said Mary. "The white ones, the dark yellow, the light yellow. In the springtime, your pap would sit up in that chair and watch them little birds all day, going in and out of his flowers."

"If they were so good, then why aren't we planting daffodils?" asked Andrew.

"They don't last through the summer, for one. But I just aint had the heart for them since we lost them in that washout," Mary replied.

"The what?"

"That whole side of the hill yonder slipped off and tore out all of this years ago. When we built it all back, I didn't want daffodils in it because I hated seeing them get killed so bad that time," said Mary.

"What caused it?" asked Andrew. "A big storm?"

"That road broke off there where the waterline runs and made a hole in the pipe, and water shot out of the side of a mountain like a big old faucet," said Mary. "Like nothing you ever saw."

She stood and pointed to a spot. "It came out right there, ran all the way past the side of the house, washed all this out and then went straight down to Troublesome Creek yonder."

Jerry finally spoke from the back porch. "She's not exaggerating. It woulda washed you away had you tried to stand in it. Hard to describe how strong it was. Like on TV when you see fire hydrants knocked over; it was just a water explosion."

Mary spoke as she placed the azalea in the hole and pushed dirt around it with her feet. "If Jerry hadn't run up and cut that main water line off, it probably would have destroyed the whole house. In a few minutes, all of this was just completely gone."

"Who fixed it back?" asked Andrew. "Who paid for it?"

"Well, the road belongs to the county, so they come and fixed the road. And the waterline belongs to the city, so the city did that," explained Mary.

"And all your stuff?" asked Andrew.

"Jerry and your papaw did it," said Mary. "Worked evenings and weekends for weeks, getting all the mud moved out of the yard. Woodrow and his boys came over a couple days and helped too. But it was mainly just them."

"Seems to me like they should have at least given you some money," said Andrew.

"They? Who is 'they' exactly?" asked Jerry from the porch.

"I don't know," said Andrew. "The city or the county. Whoever caused it, I guess."

"Ernie Wright was the county attorney back then. He came over one day and said it wasn't the county's fault because the road slipped on account of the waterline breaking," said Mary. "And then the mayor sent the water people over here and they said their waterline wouldn't have broke if the road hadn't slipped. So it wasn't their fault neither."

"They blamed each other?" Andrew asked.

"Yes," Mary answered.

"What she's not saying is that the mayor is Ernie's brother in law," said Jerry.

"Yeah, they're kin all right," said Mary.

"The mayor said it was the county's responsibility and to take it up with Ernie, and Ernie said it was a city problem and to send the bill to the mayor," said Jerry. "But neither of them were going to do a thing. They just kept pointing the finger at the other one. And when Daddy finally had enough and went to town, they was both off fishing on Lake Cumberland. Fishing together too. We figured we might as well do it ourselves."

"That's dicked up," said Andrew.

"Watch that mouth," said Mary. With gloved hands, she reached into a hot bag of red mulch and knelt to spread it around the azalea. The plastic bag had cooked in the July sun, and the sweaty mulch steamed the little plant above. "Now those daffodils all got picked up and

184

washed away when the water tore through here. But they was awful hearty plants. They grow out of little bulbs like onions, and they was awful hearty ones, those flowers of your pap's. The following spring, they come up all down yonder along Troublesome Creek. Hundreds of them, scattered all over the place. They took root wherever they landed and came up at that same spot the next year. Right around Easter time. I always called them 'Easter flowers' when I was a little girl because they always said they come up around Easter."

Mary stood again and looked out over the field of bulrush toward the creekbank. "All down through there was a path of them Easter flowers where the water had run. The ones that used to grow here in this bed. They just popped up one day, out of nowhere. Was something to see. So exciting too because we thought we lost all of them. And every year, right before Easter, that whole creekbank would be lit up with them daffodils. I'd get so excited when I'd see the first ones. Just one day they'd be all over."

Mary paused as she looked away from the bulrush and the creek. She stepped back toward Andrew and the azalea. "But then Troublesome Creek flooded real bad one year and it washed them out of that spot too. Out of that field and off the creekbank. And they was gone for good after that."

"Maybe they got washed down somewhere else and took up there," said Andrew. "Where does Troublesome Creek go?"

"I've thought about that," Mary said. "You know, you see them Easter flowers show up wild in fields and pastures and in peoples' yards all the time. Right before Easter. And they had to come from somewhere. I do think, when I see one that's the same shade of yellow or white that we had, I do think that maybe could be one of your pap's old flowers."

Jerry watched Mary and Andrew gather their gardening materials. "Are y'all about done?" he asked, as he prepared to get Andrew alone to speak to him.

"Oh, now he offers to help," said Mary. "Yes, we are."

As Jerry stepped toward Andrew to pull his nephew aside, his work phone rang.

*   *   *

An ambulance and several cars were in the driveway of Eddie's house when Jerry arrived at the home of the newspaper publisher. On the porch, Eddie and his wife, Marilyn, talked to two police officers.

As Jerry began up the steps to the porch, Deputy Tackett called to him. "Back here, Jerry."

Jerry followed the deputy into a bedroom. On the floor was the body of Eddie's twenty-two-year-old son, the young man called Little Eddie or Eddie Junior around town. Jerry knelt to look at the body. Eddie appeared in the doorway, with a red, tear-stained face.

"I tried CPR," said Eddie. "But I didn't know what I was doing."

Jerry stood to put a hand on his friend's back and looked around to see the room was a wreck. The mattress was partially off the bed and Little Eddie's chest of drawers was knocked over. Eddie had struggled to move his son and had created the disturbance with his efforts.

"I remembered that you are supposed to put them in the floor to do CPR," Eddie continued. "Not on a bed.

Doesn't work on a bed. So, I did that. I had a hard time getting him out of the bed myself. It didn't help none. I believe he was already gone."

Jerry did not respond with words, but he patted Eddie's shoulder.

The two men stepped out of the room while the body was bagged and removed. After a trip to the kitchen, where Jerry found Ale-8 in the refrigerator and convinced Eddie to have a bottle, the two walked back to the bedroom together. Jerry slid the mattress squarely back on the box springs, and Eddie sat down on it and cried.

Marilyn appeared in the door to the bedroom.

"I knew we should have done something about all that stuff he was doing. I thought he was just having fun and he'd be smart about it," said Eddie.

"You don't know what it was," said Marilyn.

"Your son. Was he using drugs? Like hard drugs? Opioids?" asked Jerry.

Eddie shook his head. Marilyn started to correct him, but Eddie told her, "Marilyn, just don't."

Marilyn glared at Eddie and walked out of the room. Eddie stood and released a long sigh. He saw the overturned chest of drawers in the bedroom floor. Eddie walked to it and attempted to return it to a standing position, but when he lifted it, the top shelf rolled out and fell into the floor. Eddie burst into tears again and sat back on the bed.

"Let me do that," Jerry said.

Jerry stood the chest upright and slid the drawer back in place. He returned the items that had fallen out, beginning with a composition book, an old flip phone, and a pack of playing cards. The last item he returned was a pale white Halloween mask, a cartoon ghost with a goofy smile, exposed pink tongue, and blue half-moons under his eyes. Jerry treated the Casper mask with the same care he gave to the other items in the drawer. He carefully placed it back in its home, where it would reside with the rest of the dead man's belongings.

* * *

"I'm telling you. Me and you will go tomorrow over to Big Branch Church," Mary said. "They have a paved driveway that goes up a little hill. All you have to do is walk up that hill backwards a few times and that thing's coming out. Works every time, walking up a hill backwards."

"I can't walk frontwards, let alone backwards," said Susie.

"Just a few steps. I'll help you," said Mary. "And pop, out it'll come."

Jerry entered the house, looking defeated.

"What is it?" Mary asked.

"Eddie and Marilyn's boy," Jerry replied. "Found him dead."

"Eddie Junior?" asked Mary. "What from?"

"Looks like he was just mixed up in the wrong stuff," said Jerry.

"I swear," said Mary. "Eddie and Marilyn. Aint two finer people in the world."

"Nope," agreed Jerry. "And these kids, they end up hurting the people around them as much as they hurt themselves."

Jerry looked at Andrew, but his nephew was not paying attention to the conversation. He had on his headphones and played a jewel-stacking game on his phone.

"Seems like all we do around here is go to funerals," said Mary. "Randy will retire a rich man with all the people he's burying these days."

"You feeling better?" Jerry asked Susie.

"Me and her are walking tomorrow," said Mary.

"I don't think I can do that," said Susie.

"We're gonna get that thing out of her yet," said Mary.

Susie put her hands on the couch and tried to lift herself to a standing position. "Can you take me back to the trailer, baby? I think I want to get back in the recliner and turn on the fan."

Jerry helped Susie walk back to the trailer and got her comfortable in the recliner.

"I hope you will be happy with just one child," said Susie. "Because I am not doing this again. I'm calling the vet and scheduling you for one of those surgeries next week."

Jerry smiled and helped his wife stretch out her legs in the recliner. He sat with Susie and watched her fall to sleep. He listened to her snore as he looked out the window toward Mary's house. His conversation with Andrew would have to wait until another day.

Jerry fell asleep on the couch, across from his wife in the recliner. After midnight, a sound woke him. He looked out and saw a large pickup truck in his mother's driveway. The driver stopped before getting near the house and killed the truck's lights. Jerry saw Betty step out of the cab. He watched his sister walk up the driveway and enter the house quietly. Jerry noticed the truck did not leave, and he felt the engine idling.

Jerry slipped out the back of his trailer and walked around to the side closest to Mary's house. He looked directly at Andrew's bedroom from the corner. A light came on in his nephew's room, and Jerry saw Betty's silhouette standing over his bed. He watched them talk, but he did not hear their conversation.

Moments after the light went off in Andrew's room, Betty came back out of the house. Her departure from the home was as careful and quiet as her arrival. She jumped in the truck's cab and smiled at her friend Leroy. "Got it. Let's go."

Leroy started to back up, but when he looked in his rearview mirror, he saw his reverse lights illuminate a figure standing in the driveway.

"What the hell?" Leroy said to Betty.

She looked behind the truck and saw Jerry, just as he fired a flashlight into the rearview mirror and temporarily blinded Leroy.

"Turn it off," ordered Jerry. "Toss the keys out."

"Who the hell?" said Leroy.

"That's my dumbass brother," Betty said. "He's a cop."

"A cop?" said Leroy. "Why didn't you tell me your brother was a cop?"

"Turn it off," said Jerry again. "And the keys. This is the last time I'm asking nicely."

Jerry appeared to carelessly shine the light all over the truck and surrounding objects, but Betty realized he was doing that to hit the windows of Mary's house, creating the disturbance that should wake anyone inside.

"Shit," she said. "He's trying to wake everyone up with that damn light."

Leroy turned off the ignition and threw the keys out the window. Mary and Andrew appeared on the front porch. Jerry picked up the keys before walking to the passenger side and opening the door.

"Give it to me," said Jerry.

"What?" asked his sister.

"Give it to me."

"You aint got nothing better to do--" began Betty.

"Give. It. To. Me," said Jerry.

Betty handed Jerry a baggie of marijuana from her purse. Jerry walked to the front of the truck so that Mary and Andrew saw him in the beams of the headlights. He opened the baggie, dumped the contents on the ground and stepped on it with his slipper.

Jerry approached Leroy and tossed the keys back. "Why don't you get out of here and take her with you," Jerry told him. "Let her stay with you tonight. If you are interested in her in that way, it'll be a guaranteed score."

"Oh God. Shut up, Jerry," said Betty.

"Look y'all, I don't know what's--" Leroy began.

Jerry interrupted, "Buddy, shut your mouth, start your truck and get out of here. You're not in any trouble, but if you open your mouth again, you're gonna be."

Leroy looked to Betty. She said, "Do it. Just go."

The truck pulled away, and Jerry walked to Mary's house. He stepped onto the porch without looking at his mother or nephew and walked through the front door.

"Jerry," said Mary.

Jerry stopped and looked back at her. "He stays out here until I'm done."

"What are you going to do?" asked Mary.

Jerry ignored her and continued into the house. He walked into Andrew's room and began tossing it like a prison guard. He flipped over the mattress, pulled out drawers and looked inside vents.

Andrew stepped into the room, with Mary behind

him.

"Aint nothing here," said Andrew.

"Jerry, what are you doing?" asked Mary.

"I told you to keep him outside, Mom. If you aint going to help me none here, then go check on Susie. I've never seen her this sick."

"Oh my Lord in Heaven," Mary said, as she darted down the hallway.

After she was gone, Jerry looked to Andrew and asked, "What else do you have in here?"

"Nothing. I just had the pot. It's not a real drug nohow. It's safer than liquor."

"I'm not looking for pot, Andrew," said Jerry. "I'm looking for the pills you took from Stanley Jennings."

"What are you talking about?"

"You know what I'm talking about," said Jerry. "If you weren't my nephew, you'd already be in jail."

"What do you think I've done?"

Jerry slowly walked over to his nephew. "I can't protect you any longer."

"Protect me? From what?"

The two heard the front door to the house slam open and Mary enter the house running.

"Jerry! Jerry, the baby's coming!"

*   *   *

"You don't need to be in there. They's some things a man just shouldn't see," Mary told her son, as they sat together in the waiting room of the Buckner County Hospital.

Jerry acknowledged her advice with a nod.

"What were you saying to Andrew?" Mary asked.

"Mom, there's things you don't know."

Mary shook her head no and dug through her purse for her lipstick. "I know what he's been up to. But he's getting things straightened out. It's been a long time since anything went missing or he's done anything bad."

"Oh yeah?"

Mary found her firetruck red stick and popped the top. "What are you getting at?"

"You don't want to know."

"Tell me," she said, as she glided the cosmetic across her lips.

"Stanley Jennings."

"What about him?"

Jerry looked to Mary. He clenched his jaw and locked eyes with her. When she saw his certainty and resolve, she looked away from her son.

"No," she said.

"You think I'm making it up?"

Mary put the lipstick back in her purse and flipped through the pockets to avoid looking at Jerry. "What proof do you have?"

"He's the only one it can be."

Mary stopped her pretend search and looked to her son in disgust. "The only one it can be? What does that even mean?"

"You and Betty not believing he could never do nothing wrong is what's turned him into who he is," said Jerry. "Y'all have always--"

Mary cut Jerry off with a stern look. "How he is aint my fault, and you know that."

"Now he's done something none of us can get him out of," said Jerry.

"He wouldn't do nothing like that," said Mary.

"He didn't mean to kill nobody. That is clear. Was probably just there to get Stanley's pain medicine from his surgery. But things got bad."

"Andrew couldn't kill nobody," Mary protested.

"You'd be surprised at what somebody can do if they don't have any options," said Jerry. "At the right time and the right place, a man is capable of almost anything."

"I don't believe you."

"Didn't expect you would," said Jerry. "And you don't have to, but it's true. Stanley died the night of the Fourth. Andrew was supposed to be with you. Was he?"

"No."

"Where was he?"

"I don't know."

"See? You just let him come and go like that?" asked Jerry. "What's wrong with you and Betty? No wonder he's into all this nonsense."

A nurse entered the waiting room, and Jerry and Mary stood.

"Congratulations."

*　　　　　*　　　　　*

Susie held the sleeping baby in a little white and pink bundle. They called her Geraldine Faye Somerset, the first name an honor to a grandfather she would never know. Mary and Jerry sat in the room with her. Mary reached into the bed and positioned Susie's hands more to her liking.

"Keep your hand under its little head right good," said Mary. "Its little neck aint strong at all."

Susie's heavy eyes struggled to stay open. "I feel like I'm about to go to sleep. One of you want her?"

Mary stood quickly and scooped up the baby. She

walked away from the bed and sat in a big chair in the corner. "Aint it the prettiest little thing that ever was. Looks just like her daddy." She saw the big, curious eyes looking up at her layers of vibrant lipstick and said to the baby, "Yes, her does. Yes, her does."

Jerry stood and walked over to Susie. He touched her hands and forehead as she slept. He looked to his mother and daughter.

"Happy to have a granddaughter this time?"

"Yes," said Mary. "It sure has been a long time since we had a little one."

Mary played with the baby's hands and fingers. She made silly faces and was happy when she got a reaction. She looked at Jerry and saw him gazing out the window into the dark night. "That boy didn't do what you say. You gotta stand by your people, Jerry. If you aint got family--"

Jerry did not let her finish. "This is my job, Mom. Standing by my people means failing at my job. They are talking about me for sheriff, Mom. Sheriff."

"They should," said Mary. "You earned it a long time ago. They never should have put that boy in over you because of his daddy."

"You see? This is my chance," said Jerry. "I gotta do my job right and not bend the rules. And it's more than just me now. I have a new family of my own, and I have to make choices for them. What's best for us."

Jerry turned away from the window.

"You better not think you're coming over here to get this little thing away from me," said Mary. "I aint done holding it yet."

Jerry smiled at her. "Oh no. You can tend to her for a while. I'm going to run down to the car and check in with the station."

Jerry left the room and walked out to the hospital's parking lot. He arrived at his car and looked back at the darkened windows on the building's third floor. One room was lit up. Inside he saw the ceiling tiles and the bluish glare of the fluorescent lights, but he could not see his wife or his new child. He knew they were in there though, and he knew they were resting.

*　　　　　*　　　　　*

Jerry was alone in Mary's living room. He toggled between sitting on the couch and pacing. When he walked around the living room and kitchen, his head was down, as he contemplated his options.

At around 4 a.m., he made the slow walk to Andrew's room. The boy lay sleeping in his bed, one arm hanging off the side. Jerry woke his nephew by sliding a handcuff on the wrist of that arm and closing it tight.

"What are you doing?" Andrew said, struggling to get away from his uncle.

"I can't let you destroy my family, Andrew," Jerry replied.

"What do you mean?"

"I've done all I can do for you," said Jerry. "You've made your choices and now you have to pay for what you did."

Jerry held the other handcuff and walked out of the room. Andrew had no choice but to go with his uncle. When he struggled, Jerry pulled harder, and the handcuff bit his wrist to the bone.

"You're hurting me." Andrew pleaded with his uncle. "All this over some pot?"

Jerry did not answer. He pulled out his phone and

dialed the sheriff's voicemail.

"Sheriff, this is Jerry. Listen, I'm bringing in my nephew for the murder of Stanley Jennings."

"Murder?!" shouted Andrew.

"When you get in, he'll be in one of the holding cells," Jerry continued, as he pulled Andrew out of the house and onto the porch. "I reckon I've avoided the obvious here and tried to figure out a way where he wasn't involved."

"I didn't do none of this," said Andrew.

"But I've got to accept it," said Jerry. "I wanna do whatever I can to help him, but I can't break the law for him."

"What are you talking about?" Andrew said.

"I mean, I can't break it no more," Jerry said. He pulled Andrew down the steps. "There's been some things I've done wrong here. You and your daddy have got to decide about that. But we can figure it all out later."

"I did not kill nobody," said Andrew. "Why won't you believe me?"

Jerry hung up. He put the phone away and ragdolled Andrew into the back of his patrol car. "I'm done with the lies, Andrew," he said. "You could at least be honest with me. I know you didn't mean to kill that man. Get you a good lawyer and you might just serve a couple years for manslaughter. Heck, you might even could walk since I've done such a bad job with this case. But stop the lies."

"I am being honest with you," said Andrew. "I didn't kill nobody. I swear. And I would tell you if I had."

"Then tell me."

"But I didn't," said Andrew. "I would tell you,

because you're the only person in this whole world who means anything to me. You and Maw. Lord knows my mommy and daddy aint no count. If you don't believe in me, then I might as well done killed somebody."

"Where were you the Fourth of July? All day and at the fireworks? You were supposed to be with Mom, but you weren't there and you weren't here all day."

"I was somewhere else," said Andrew.

"Where?"

"Just trust me. I didn't do it, but I can't tell you where I was."

"You just said you would tell me if you killed someone, but you can't tell me where you were on the Fourth?"

"Yeah."

"That makes no sense, Andrew. And you know who tells me stories that make no sense in the back of this car?"

"Who?"

"Guilty people."

Jerry waited for a reply from the backseat of his car, but nothing came. He looked in the rearview mirror and saw the blank gaze in Andrew he had seen before. As with other people Jerry drove to jail, Andrew now appeared resigned to his predicament. The young man searched for agency and dignity found only in the acceptance of failure. He realized that everything he ever dreamed about or wanted ended in this slow drive to the police station. His grandmother would never look at him the same. His uncle had abandoned him. Judges and probation officers who had given him one more chance would not have room for additional sympathy. Andrew always sought soft shoulders and friendly ears in others, and he knew those were not found on the journey ahead.

∗   ∗   ∗

Susie held the baby as Jerry entered the hospital room. Mary stood in the corner with her arms crossed.

"Where'd you go?" Mary asked.

"I woke up and you weren't here," said Susie.

"Did you go to the house?" asked Mary.

"Yes," said Jerry.

"Andrew?"

"Yes."

"Where is he?" Mary asked.

"In jail, where he belongs."

"In jail?!" cried Susie.

"Take me to him," said Mary.

Jerry looked out the window and motioned his head toward the rays of sunshine coming over the mountains. "The sheriff will be there in a couple hours, around eight or so. He'll book him. We can go see him after that."

"Why is he in jail? What's going on?" asked Susie.

"Take me now," said Mary. "I want to see him."

"Mom, there's no need--" Jerry began.

"Now!"

Jerry and Mary left Susie and the baby at the hospital, and Jerry drove them the five miles to the police station. No words passed between them. As Jerry pulled into a parking space, Mary opened her door with the car still rolling to a stop. She stumbled out, gained her balance and double-stepped toward the entrance.

"You can't get in without me," Jerry yelled to her through the window.

Undaunted, Mary continued to the entrance and beat

on the glass door when she arrived. Jerry came behind her and swiped his badge to authorize the door. As she tried to open it, Jerry held it. "I know you're mad, but you gotta settle down. If you go stomping into a police station, you're liable to get shot."

She looked at him and nodded agreement. Jerry let her pass and she disappeared in the direction of the overnight desk.

Jerry started to follow his mother, but he saw Little Dan pull into the parking lot and exit his vehicle.

"I listened to your message at home. I wish you'd called me before you did anything," said Little Dan, walking to the entrance.

"I'm sorry."

Mary yelled from inside. "Jerry? Get in here!"

Jerry and Little Dan walked toward the overnight desk. The officer stood in front of Mary and would not allow her to pass him.

"Would you tell this person I want to see my grandson?" Mary demanded.

"I told her, no visitors at this hour," the officer said.

"Go ahead, but go with her," Little Dan said.

The officer opened a box for Mary and had her empty her belongings inside.

"Are you sure it's him?" Little Dan asked Jerry.

Mary heard the question from the desk and answered, "It absolutely is not him."

The men ignored her. Little Dan continued, "I wish you would've let me decide if the evidence was there before you brought him in."

"I'm sorry," said Jerry. "I know I screwed this up."

"You sure did!" Mary yelled at him.

"Get her out of here," Jerry barked to the officer.

"Sir?"

"If she wants to go see him, take her back to see him."

The officer held up a paper and began, "But she needs to fill out--"

"Take her now, Goddamnit!" Jerry interrupted.

"Just do it," said Little Dan.

Mary and the officer left the reception area. Jerry turned to Little Dan and said, "I was trying to protect him. But I realized tonight that I wasn't doing right and I needed to do what was best for my wife and myself. And my little girl."

"Jerry, that's all the more reason for you to have settled down, thought this through. You aren't looking at the bigger picture here."

From the cell wing, Jerry heard a sound that he would carry with him the rest of his life. His mother, screaming a scream that no person should ever release. The sound coming from her was rage and loss and desperation and disbelief. It grew out of a deep cavern in her gut and erupted to paint the walls of the cell wing and the rest of the police station. The jail felt smaller as she screamed, and the temperature inside rose. Time slowed for the sound to fill every corner of the building, before it died a slow, fading death, the last cries and whimpers bouncing off the cinder block walls and racing to her son.

"No," said Little Dan, as he watched Jerry dash down the hallway toward his mother. "Oh God, no."

*   *   *

"No man knows what the sleeper knows. Nor is it for us to judge what lies between him and Thee," Preacher Bryant said before his packed church.

Andrew's open casket was in front of the preacher, between the lectern and the church's first pews. The man of God continued, "I like to believe a merciful Lord won't judge a man based on one bad choice. Those who knew young Andrew knew him to be a kind, gentle soul. But he had challenges. He turned in the direction of God and was taking steps toward embracing him fully. But he got sidetracked. While many judge him for the mistakes he made and the pain they'll say he caused, I like to believe God sees the total man that Andrew could have been and the good things he would have done in life. And if God judges that Andrew, he'll find a place for him in his kingdom."

Among the sniffles and open weeps, a few people called "Amen" to Preacher Bryant. He nodded in acknowledgement. The preacher looked into the choir and said, "Brother Calhoun."

Big Dan stood in the choir and walked to the lectern. He bowed slightly in reverence to Betty and Mary, seated in the corner of the right front pew. He did the same to Jerry and Susie in the opposite pew. Big Dan would have acknowledged members of Andrew's family from his father's side, but he was told before the event that none would be in attendance.

Big Dan clasped his hands in front of him at his waist and took a deep breath. He began. He did not sing with the choir this time. He held the song himself and sang about a poor wayfaring stranger going home over the River Jordan. The members of the church heard about traveling through dark clouds in a world of woe. If Andrew roamed with the stranger from Big Dan's song, he traveled to a land of beautiful fields, with no sickness, toil or danger. A bright land, into which he did go.

CHAPTER 10

I thought about my dad when Little Dan won the election to go to State Congress. I don't know what he would have thought of that night. Me and Susie attended the victory party at the mayor's house. They had paper lanterns on string lines all over the outside of his estate. Those things put out so much light you could see the party reflecting in the lake down below. Me and Susie stood on a terrace and looked down at the party and at the houseboats on the lake. We couldn't believe we were there.

In the backyard, white folding chairs faced a stage where Little Dan made his speech. His daddy spoke first though and let everybody know Little Dan would not be a State Congressman long. US Senator or Governor would be their target in the next ten years.

Me and Susie actually walked to the party. We walked to the mayor's house just a few hundred yards from our home. That still don't feel real. We only had a few things in the new house by then, but we attended the party and spent our first night in that place after it was over. We walked home too. Walked, from the mayor's house on Woodland Estates. It's just so hard to believe.

Little Dan's brother, Steven, was already back from the Navy by then. Apparently, he had a problem with a drug test, and they sent him home real quick. He spent that night of the election telling the daughters of Buckner County's elite families how he would have unique access to the new congressman. He also told them about his new job in management of an oil and gas company Big Dan partially owned.

Little Dan mentioned me by name when he was on stage, said I'd take over the next day as interim sheriff. I didn't think it would happen that quick. For the rest of the night, people just started calling me "Sheriff" like that's my name. No more "Jerry" and not even "Sheriff Somerset." Just "Sheriff." I hear it forty or fifty times per day now.

So yeah, I think about what Dad would have said had he been there or what he'd think about people calling me "Sheriff." At forty, I'm a little older now than he was when he died, and I realized the other day I have been without a father for longer than I had one. But what he would have thought about all the stuff that has gone on in this family still matters to me, and I think about him seeing me up there at Woodland Estates under them strings of paper lanterns.

*   *   *

At Calhoun's Restaurant, Jerry left Big Dan, the mayor and the county judge executive to continue with their week's work. As he passed the buffet, one of the workers called to him. "You want to take some of them cinnamon rolls home to Susie? I can box them up for you."

"No thanks," said Jerry. "Not sure when I'll be home, and I don't want to drive around with them all day."

"Oh, I understand. I'd eat them all for sure if it was me."

Jerry forced a smile and left. He stopped by his old trailer to pick up some boxes and totes to take to the new house. His plan was to drop them off with Susie and resume his work for the day.

When he arrived at the new house, Jerry found Susie in the dining room, placing her grandmother's China tableware in a glass-doored hutch that came with the house. Each piece of the set had a brass rim and small lavender roses trailing over the glazed stoneware.

"This thing is huge," Susie said of the hutch. "I need to see if Mom has more things she can give me to display in here. I think she's got a couple of them big pitcher-and-cups sets, like for tea or lemonade. One of them would look good in the middle if it's a plain color and not too gaudy."

"Aint it a little dark in here for you?" Jerry asked as he flipped a light switch.

"Wait!" Susie yelled. "That's not the light. That turns off the outlet for the microwave."

"Oh."

Jerry turned the switch back. Susie stepped into the kitchen and saw the clock on the microwave now flashing 12:00.

"I've had to set that thing three times now," Susie said. "I keep forgetting not to use that switch. And I have to look up every time about how to set that clock."

Susie shuffled through paperwork in a utility drawer and said, "Now where is that book?"

Jerry looked at the switch and then into the kitchen. "Why would this switch work on something in there?"

"I don't know," said Susie. "But it does. There's another one like that upstairs. The one that should turn on the light in the hallway actually turns a light on and off in the little bedroom."

"That don't make no sense at all." Jerry scanned the walls and ceiling, unimpressed. "Maybe this isn't so great after all."

"It's just a couple switches, honey. You could get somebody to fix them."

As Jerry walked around the dining room, he looked down at the floor. "And do you hear that creaking?"

He bounced up and down on the hardwood, repeating the sound.

"I don't hear anything," Susie said.

"Big Dan didn't mention any of this."

"Jerry, stop looking our gift house in the mouth."

"If I knew all this," Jerry paused. "I don't know. This deal, I just don't know.

Susie looked at Jerry confused. "I would never want to go back to the way things were."

"The way things were? Like when my mother still spoke to me? And my nephew was still alive? Why would I ever want to go back to those things?"

"What?" Susie said. "How does any of that have anything to do with this?"

Jerry shook his head and left the room. Susie secured her dishes and went after him.

"Hey, come back here," she called. "You can't just say something like that and turn your back on me."

"I know you wouldn't want to go back to the way those things used to be," Jerry said. "Why would you? But I sure wish I could. I don't expect you to feel about it the way I do."

"That is not fair, Jerry Somerset. Not fair at all. I'm sorry all that happened to you, but this house and our new life doesn't have nothing to do with those things."

"It doesn't?"

"Why are you saying that?"

"Never knew a free house and a raise at work would cost us so much. Or at least cost me so much."

"Don't say that again," Susie demanded. "Don't you

dare say you went through all that alone. You've said it twice now, and I will let that slide, but you better never say that to me again."

"Okay, it's not just me," Jerry said. "We both got the house we wanted and the big job for me we both wanted, but I had to lose my family. I guess it's a fair trade. My family for all that."

"Are you trying to hurt me? If so, it's working."

Jerry turned away from his wife and walked toward the living room, but Susie followed. She caught him, grabbed his arm and spun him toward her. "I told you not to walk away from me like that."

"I was trying so hard to make things better for this family, and I ignored the one person who needed me the most. I didn't see it. It was right there. He needed me, and I didn't see it because I was trying to be an important man around town. I should have been happy just being Deputy Jerry, the man who lives in a trailer, hunts elk and raises turkeys."

Jerry grabbed a coat and his keys at the door.

"Where are you going? You can't just leave."

"I'm sheriff now. Remember? It's why you live in this big house. Sheriffs have work to do."

Susie stood frozen and watched Jerry put on his jacket. She did not know what more to offer the conversation to follow those remarks.

"And tonight. Big Dan says there's some guys I got to meet," Jerry said. "They'll contribute to my campaign. Not sure when I'll be home. I'll grab something at Sanderson's."

"Campaign? The election was just a few weeks ago. They just made you sheriff."

"I'm interim sheriff. I will have to run in the primaries in five months and again next November to remove 'interim' from my title."

"You'll be running unopposed."

"Maybe, but I still gotta be there tonight. Big Dan says so."

Jerry spent the rest of the day at the office, approving reports filed by his deputies. In the evening, he met Big Dan and two contractors from Louisiana at the picnic area by the lake.

"Now these old boys can't vote for you," said Big Dan. "But they're awful eager to contribute to your campaign. I told them all about you, and they said they feel safer working in a county with a feller like you in charge."

"Thanks," Jerry said and gave each man a firm handshake.

"But they don't know anybody up here. Reckon you could give them boys your private phone number and have them call you if they run into any trouble with anybody? Folks snooping around their construction site, stuff like that?"

"Absolutely. What are you guys going to be doing here?"

One of the men looked to Big Dan and received a nod of permission. "We're putting in a new marina."

"Nobody knows yet, Jerry," said Big Dan. "It'll take a year to even get it started, so we're keeping it quiet. We don't want people panicking and trying to get new dock slips. Best wait and tell everybody things when they need to know them."

Jerry gave the men his phone number and left them alone with Big Dan. He drove to Sanderson's Café, a small diner that was Calhoun's one restaurant competition. Jerry had made Sanderson's a second office since becoming sheriff; he occupied one of the corner booths before work and drank his morning coffee while reading the paper. People soon learned if they needed a word with the new sheriff, he was found at Sanderson's for a few minutes each morning. They came to tell him about their neighbor's barking dog or the sketchy person who knocked on their door and asked for money for the poor.

"I'll look into it," Jerry would say. When he asked to settle his bill each morning, he was always told one of those citizens had bought the coffee for him.

Some evenings, Jerry returned to Sanderson's to have his dinner instead of going home to Susie. He kept a composition book with him and would occasionally scribble in it, giving people the impression he was working. He mainly just doodled or wrote the same word multiple times, but people left him alone.

On this night, for the first time since he was married, Jerry considered going to see Jennifer in a capacity beyond discussing open police cases. He knew what was available there, and he knew he could lose himself with her, if for only a moment in time. He allowed that thought to stay with him while he wrote her name in his book several times.

But he decided one trip there would not be enough, and if he reopened that door, the house would eventually collapse around him. If Jennifer was more reliable, he thought maybe. But he knew she was someone not to be trusted. If he started it up with her again and she needed to use him to get something she wanted, he knew she would do it without considering how it would affect him.

He tore out the sheet with her name on it, looked at his watch and decided it was not too late to make one more trip to the trailer to get another carload of belongings.

*   *   *

Jerry put the last tote in his car and walked next door to his mother's house. He stepped up the stairs and saw that only her screen door was closed. She sat in the living room, working on a quilt, the sawtooth star design. Her stars had earth-toned centers, with bright orange legs. She intended to drape the quilt over her couch during the months of October and November, as a match for her fall decorations.

Jerry paused at the screen door and gently knocked.

"It's open," his mother called.

Jerry walked in and stood in the middle of the room. "I was just getting another load of stuff. Two more trips should get it."

Mary did not look up. "Mm-hmm."

"So, elk season starts Saturday. It's gonna be cold. I remember Daddy using a pair of camouflage gloves back when he hunted."

"How am I supposed to know where something like that is?" she asked. "If we've even still got it."

"I know where they are," Jerry said. "They're in the bottom of the gun case."

"And?"

"And I wondered if I could use them Saturday. It's gonna be cold, like I said."

"I don't know why you'd think you have to ask me for permission to use your daddy's gloves, but yeah, go ahead."

Jerry retrieved the gloves from his father's otherwise empty gun case. He walked back to the living room with his mother. "Got them."

"Mm-hmm." She still did not look at her son.

Jerry walked toward his mother. "Anything else you need?" she asked and looked up as she felt him close to her. She saw he was not looking back at her though. He stopped frozen in front of the Paul Brett Johnson baptism painting that Mary had in her house for decades.

"Stanley Jennings had that painting in his house, in his kitchen," Jerry said. His eyes searched for the man on the bridge, and Jerry flirted with the possibility that the watcher would not be in this print, that he was somehow frozen in the version on Stanley's wall and would be gone from his mother's copy. But he found the man in the nice suit and said to himself, "There he is."

"A lot of people have that painting," Mary said. "They was real popular around here when they came out."

"Stanley had it. And he died under it. His head was about right here," Jerry said and showed with his hands how low below the painting Stanley's body rested.

"Nobody wants to know those things, Jerry. Don't tell me things like that."

"I've wondered if he crawled to be under this painting," Jerry said. "Maybe it meant something to him. Or maybe he was trying to get through the kitchen and this was just the end of the line."

Mary finally put down her quilt and looked to her son. "Maybe if you had thought more about the case instead of that painting, you would have known Andrew didn't do what you said."

"I can't keep having this conversation, Mom," Jerry said and began toward the door.

"Fine," she said and picked up her quilt to continue

work.

Jerry stopped at the door. "Why don't you at least go over and see Susie and your granddaughter? She asks me all the time when you are going to come see it."

"Oh, I'm sure that pretty wife of yours is happy in that big house without me. She don't want me over there, and if she wants that baby to see it's mamaw, she knows where I live."

Jerry shook his head and left. He walked out to his car and began to back out of the driveway. Betty pulled in and got out of her car. She walked toward the door of the house. Jerry exited his vehicle and walked to her. "Hey," he said to his sister.

"Don't talk to me, Jerry."

"Why don't you and Mom come over and see Susie and the baby?" he asked.

"I said don't talk to me."

"You're blaming me for all this too, I guess," Jerry said.

"Uh, yeah. Obviously. You aint nearly as smart as you think you are, big brother."

"What does that mean?"

"You don't know nothing about what Andrew did and didn't do," Betty said. "He sure didn't kill that feller, that's for sure."

"You're wrong," said Jerry. "It was an accident, but he sure done it."

"No, he did not. And once you gave up on him, that must have just plum killed his soul. He killed himself because you stopped believing in him, dumbass. Not because he killed nobody."

"How do you know he didn't do it?" he asked her. "Did you do it?"

"No."

"Do you know who did it?" Jerry asked.

"No. But it sure wasn't him."

"How can you know that?"

Betty walked up the steps of the house. Jerry leaped onto the porch and got in front of her.

"Jerry, what in the world are you doing?" Mary called from the house.

Jerry looked into his sister's eyes. "How can you know he didn't do it?"

"You don't really wanna know."

"Yes, I do."

"All right," said Betty. "You asked."

Betty stepped off the porch and walked away from the house. She looked to her brother to follow. Jerry realized Betty did not want to tell him so close to their mother, so he went to his sister.

In a whisper, Betty said, "Andrew was with me in Florida on the Fourth of July. That whole day. We didn't get back till real late. Y'all were still at the fireworks or eating pie or whatever when we got home. And then you and him built that turkey thing when you got here."

"What? You were in Florida?"

"Yeah," said Betty. "Starla sees them doctors down there, and she don't have no driver's license. So, I told her I could take her, and I got him to go with me to help drive. She gave us both a hundred dollars, plus she gave me a few of her pills for when I get that pain in my leg."

"You took your son on a drug run?" he asked.

"Not a drug run. It's legit. She's got prescriptions, Jerry," said Betty. "She was in a car wreck when she was little and she has a bad back. And she's got nervous problems. She's got a prescription for her nervous problems too."

"How long were you there?"

"We wasn't in Florida but a couple hours. Starla came by and got us after Mom went to bed the night before. We drove through the night. Takes about nine hours. We saw them doctors and was heading back before noon. When we got back here and turned off the interstate, we actually saw the fireworks over at the football field. I came in and went straight to sleep, but Andrew wanted to surprise you by getting started in the backyard."

"How many doctors did she see down there?"

"Just four."

"Jesus Christ," said Jerry. "That's illegal. You can't go to four doctors for the same thing."

"What, you gonna arrest us all now? Oh wait, you can't. Andrew's dead."

"So that's why Andrew wouldn't tell me what he was doing," said Jerry. "He was trying to look out for his dopehead mom."

"Oh, go to hell, Jerry," said Betty. "I'm not a dopehead. This aint on me. This is on you. You think you're so smart and so moral, looking down on me and everybody else. Just think about what you did to him. Think about what Andrew must have been thinking in that cell before he killed hisself. He knew who put him there. He wasn't thinking about me, Sheriff Somerset. He was only thinking about you."

Betty pushed Jerry aside and stomped toward the door. Jerry turned to see his mother waiting for her. Jerry heard Mary say, "What were you telling him?"

Betty continued into the house and Mary shut the door, not looking at her son.

*   *   *

Jerry drove around, not wanting to go home. He told himself he was doing his duty by driving around his county. It was his county, right? He was the sheriff, the chief law enforcement officer over thousands of people. There was nothing wrong with such a man driving around and keeping an eye on things.

He drove until he was confident Susie had the baby put down for the night and was in bed herself. He contemplated not going home at all. He passed Jennifer's trailer several times. At each pass, an urge consumed him to stop. Just go knock on that door and in five minutes all the troubles of the day would be gone. He gave his turn signal once, but as he neared the trailer park, he gunned the accelerator and headed toward Woodland Estates.

When he arrived, the house was quiet. He carried in boxes by porchlight and placed them on the same bar where Big Dan had him unroll the Beretta. On his third trip, as he walked into the kitchen, Susie stood there in her robe and pink bunny house shoes.

"Do you know what's in these boxes?" she asked.

"No. I just picked them up."

"I'll figure it out in the morning. I'd rather you put them in the room where they're going, but if you don't know what's in them, I aint gonna start opening them tonight."

Susie turned to leave the room. She passed the kitchen table and saw the camouflage gloves.

"What are these?" she asked.

"Those were Daddy's gloves."

"I almost didn't see them."

"Because they're camouflage," Jerry said. "I get it."

Susie looked to him, smiled and allowed a fleeting moment of tenderness to pass between them.

"Were they in the trailer?" she asked. "I don't remember them."

"No. I got them from mom. It's going to be cold Saturday, so I need them."

"What's Saturday?"

"Elk season starts Saturday."

"I didn't know you were still going to do that."

"Why wouldn't I?"

"I don't know, Jerry. You never talk to me no more except to fight. I don't know what's going on with you."

Susie left and returned to the bedroom. Jerry made a bed on the couch in the parlor, and as was common in recent months, he did not sleep. He just faded in and out of dreams, allowing his cognizant thoughts to mix with the imagination and buried memories retrieved during dozing. Several times during the night, he reached over and touched the pool table beside the couch. His arm was just long enough and the table was just close enough that he reached the felt strip on the rail while stretched out. He rubbed the felt while dozing and while thinking about his life and his future.

As always, Jerry's thoughts returned to Andrew and the case of Stanley Jennings. He thought about the times he should have asked his nephew about that night and failed. He thought about what his sister told him. And he thought about the other members of Stanley's teams that could be suspects. One boy was in San Diego, one at the University of Florida. The young man in the woods who played the dulcimer beautifully could not be involved. Neither could Clyde, because of his ankle bracelet. Benny was at a Cincinnati Reds game, and one kid ran off to Ohio, never to return. There were those men that Little Dan marked off the list, names he omitted because he knew them all to be good boys who would not be involved in such a crime. Jerry thought about those names. The only one he remembered with certainty was Eddie's son, but Little Dan assured him Eddie's son would not have been involved in stealing drugs.

"Wait, Eddie Junior!" Jerry said, as he remembered the overdose and the regrets of Eddie and Marilyn. He looked at the clock. It was only a little after four, but he knew he would not be able to sleep. He put on his uniform and drove to the office.

At the police station, Jerry pulled the crime scene reports and autopsies related to Stanley Jennings and Eddie Junior. He wanted to check if the type of drugs stolen from Stanley's house matched what was found in Eddie Junior. When Jerry pulled Little Eddie's files, he did not find his report. Instead, a different summary was in its place, signed by Sheriff Dan Calhoun.

Jerry read Little Dan's report. He saw no mention of the drugs they found at the crime scene and no reference to the toxicology report produced after his death. Every page in the folder on Eddie Junior's death was written by Little Dan, and there were no references to opioids in anything. Someone pulling the case for the first time could have understood Little Eddie's death to have been caused by a sudden embolism or an accident.

"No coffee this morning?" the station administrative assistant, Sharlene, said when she looked in on Jerry.

"Huh?"

"Word's getting around that you have your coffee over at Sanderson's. They say folks go there to talk to you. Say it's like seeing the Pope."

Jerry felt defensive. "I just want to give people a way

to--"

Sharlene saw his discomfort and interrupted. "Oh, it's not a bad thing, Sheriff. People like the access. The whole county loves you and thinks you're doing a fine job."

"Thank you."

Sharlene leaned in and whispered, "Best damn sheriff we've had in a long time if you ask me."

"Again, thank you."

"It was just odd seeing you here this early. I'll let you get back to work."

Jerry next searched the backup files in the basement. Locked in a weatherproof vault, the information for Eddie Junior was the same as the main files, all pages written by Little Dan. Jerry accessed the online records. Everything was the same. The original reports, written by Jerry, were gone.

Gone, as in forever.

*   *   *

"Hey Sheriff. You're out early," said Eddie when Jerry entered his office. Eddie was filling a glass bowl on top of a bookshelf with chestnuts from a brown bag. "These are my last ones of the year. Gathered them out of the backyard."

He offered the bag, but Jerry shook his head no.

"I guess you got chestnut trees all over, huh?" Eddie said and took a seat at his desk.

Jerry sat on the other side and said nothing.

"What is it, Jerry?"

"I want you to tell me the truth, Eddie," said Jerry.

"Okay, sure. Anything."

"Did your boy kill Stanley Jennings?" asked Jerry.

"Kill? Stanley? What?"

"And did you know? And that day, here in this office, did you let me think my nephew might have done it because it'd get the heat off your son?"

Eddie fidgeted and squirmed in his chair, as Jerry glared at him. Eddie could not return Jerry's look, instead he scanned the room. He felt Jerry's eyes on him and stood from his desk. He turned his back and walked to the window behind him.

Jerry let Eddie stand at the window for several minutes. He saw Eddie scratch his nose and rub his forehead multiple times, as he pondered what to say. Eddie finally let out a long sigh and turned to see Jerry still locked on him. The newspaperman returned to his seat and dissolved from confusion and bewilderment into resignation and defeat. "I'm sorry, Jerry."

"What do you mean?"

"Wasn't supposed to go like this."

"How was it supposed to go?"

"He didn't do anything, Jerry. Andrew didn't do anything."

"I know that now."

"But you didn't then?"

"No, I didn't know that then, but I'm guessing you did."

"I couldn't tell you."

"Why not?"

"Because I was protecting my son. I couldn't tell you your nephew wasn't involved without telling you my boy did it."

"Why didn't you tell me after he died? I realize that was a hard time for you, but I was right there in your house. You could have ended the entire investigation right there. And my nephew would still be alive."

"No, it wouldn't have ended anything."

"Why not?"

"Because it wasn't just my son who was there."

"Someone else too?"

"Yes."

"Another young man from another well-connected family who plays by a different set of rules and has his daddy clean up his messes for him?"

"I guess you already know," Eddie said.

"I've got a pretty good idea. Little Dan knew all along too?"

"I didn't say that," said Eddie. "I didn't say nobody's name."

"Why not? Why won't you say that? You just said you were sorry about all of this, but are you not willing even now to do and say the right thing?"

"Jerry, I just run the newspaper. I gave up long ago believing I could make a difference here. I give people the weather forecast, and if someone grows a big pumpkin, I take a picture of it and write about it. But what am I going to do to actually change the way things work around here?"

Jerry looked at him in disgust.

Eddie continued, "If I had just come out with the truth, my boy would be alive. He'd be in prison for a long time, but he'd still be alive. And Andrew, he'd be alive too."

Jerry stood and walked around the office. He looked back at Eddie. "Y'all just decided to frame Andrew on the spot? That don't make no sense."

"No. For a couple days, we didn't know what to do. We were all scared to death of you because you were on the case so hard. But then, well, apparently you made a list at work of potential suspects. And the way I understand it, you left your nephew off the list. Like you was hiding something."

"Jesus. He saw me do that? He saw that right off?"

Eddie nodded. "He had you. He knew where your head was. He knew you were scrambling to save Andrew, so it was easy to make you think Andrew had done it. And keep you away from our boys."

Jerry walked toward Eddie's desk.

"Before you arrest me--" Eddie began.

"Arrest you?" Jerry interrupted. "I ought to just shoot you. Seems like it's nothing to cover up murders around here."

"Well?" asked Eddie.

"What?"

"Are you?"

"Am I what?"

"Gonna shoot me?" asked Eddie.

"No, you dumbass," said Jerry. "But stand up for me."

"Why?"

Jerry glared at Eddie.

"Okay," Eddie said and stood in front of Jerry.

"You got any weapons on you?"

"No."

"I need to check, so slowly turn around and let me see your beltline."

Eddie did as he was told and stood with his back to Jerry.

"Good," said Jerry. "Now slowly turn back to me."

Eddie moved to turn over his right shoulder.

"Nope, the other way," Jerry said.

Eddie stopped and turned counterclockwise.

"Slowly," said Jerry.

Eddie slowed his movement. When he was halfway

turned back, his chin was visible to Jerry over Eddie's left shoulder. With a closed fist, the sheriff threw a right cross that connected on the chin and dropped Eddie to the floor. Motionless as soon as he flopped against the fake hardwood, Eddie began a peaceful snore and looked like a dog sleeping under a shade tree.

Jerry pulled a chair beside Eddie and sat down. He thought about what he had just learned, what Eddie told him. He understood why Little Dan had sent Jerry to the newspaper office initially and why the police reports were now missing. He also understood why Little Dan told him not to ask for help from the State Police. But one thing remained that he did not understand.

"Jerry?" Eddie's faint voice said from the floor.

Jerry stood and looked at him. "Do you know why you're in the floor?"

"Yes," Eddie struggled to speak. He pressed his hand against his chin and cheek, trying to work out the pain. "I think it's broken."

"If I hear you've told anyone about our conversation today, I will do much worse than this. I swear to God, do not test me. I will put you in the hospital for a very long time."

"Yes sir," Eddie said softly and flinched. He pressed on his jaw harder.

"I don't know what I'm going to do with you. I've got to think about it."

Eddie said nothing.

"But while you were out, I ran through all of this, and one thing bothers me."

"Yeah?"

"It wasn't just the blood on the wall and the team picture and the drugs that convinced me to arrest

Andrew."

Eddie leaned up and rested against his desk. He looked to Jerry and said softly, "The woman?"

"What?" Jerry said.

"One of them Walker girls, I understand. Apparently, you have something with her. They needed her to pass you some bad information on Andrew, and she needed them to get her son out of foster care. Bring him home to her."

"They did that?"

Eddie nodded. Jerry placed a hand on Eddie's desk as he bent at the waist. He steadied himself as the life fled from his legs and his knees buckled. He searched for words. "That's coldblooded. Coldblooded of them to go to her and make an offer like that."

"They did seek her out, but it wasn't to make an offer or anything. They just went there to ask her what she knew about what you were thinking of the case. The Calhouns didn't come up with the arrangement for her to lie to you to get her son back, Jerry."

"Then who did?"

"The woman," Eddie whispered. "The woman. They say she missed that boy."

*　　　*　　　*

Big Dan stood between Doctor Wilma Murphy and Nurse Practitioner Joseph Akers as he announced to the people before him the specifics of Buckner County's new drug rehab center. Jerry stood in the back and listened to Big Dan's short speech about the need of the county to address prescription drug abuse. He said every family in Buckner County could claim opioids had affected them in some way, including the

Calhoun family.

Big Dan turned the presentation over to Doctor Murphy. She thanked Big Dan for the donation that made the center possible and for convincing her to relocate from Maryland, where she had spent the last decade of her life in one of the largest rehab centers in the country. Doctor Murphy claimed to be one of the most published authors in the world on the topic of opioids in Appalachia, and now she was going to apply her expertise to Buckner County.

After the speeches, Big Dan brought the two new faces to meet Jerry. "Jerry is the finest sheriff not named Calhoun this county has ever seen," Big Dan told the two.

As Jerry shook their hands, he felt the snap of a camera behind and turned to see Eddie taking pictures for the newspaper.

"Let's not get the sheriff in one for the paper, Ed," Big Dan said. "Don't want people associating law enforcement with this place. They shouldn't be scared to come here."

Jerry looked to Eddie as he stepped out of the way for another picture, but he did not receive a look in return. After taking the last photo, Eddie packed his camera away and left.

Big Dan stepped back to Jerry and said, "I'm taking Wilma and Joe here up to Calhoun's tonight. Probably gonna break out some of them nice steaks. You wanna come?"

"Probably shouldn't," Jerry answered.

"Oh, I see what's going on," Big Dan said.

"You do?"

"Yeah, you're getting in bed early tonight because you think you're going to get the biggest elk in the morning if you get plenty of sleep. You aint fooling me."

Jerry forced a smile.

*   *   *

Jerry stretched out on the couch in the parlor and closed his eyes. When he opened them, Susie stood by his feet.

"We're not doing this," she said. "I don't know what's going on, but I have put too much into this marriage. If it's some other woman, tell me. But whatever it is, we are not starting down this road."

"It's not a woman," he said.

"I wish it was," Susie said. "I could run her off, but I don't know what to do about whatever is going on."

Jerry sat up in the couch and Susie joined him. She put her arm around his waist and rested her head on his shoulder.

"Talk to me," she pleaded.

"How is she?"

"Do you mean your baby daughter that you never see?"

"Yes."

"She's fine. We watched that RuPaul makeover show together today. She loved it."

Jerry looked down at her face against his arm. She caught his chin with her hand and held it long enough to kiss him.

"I can tell she's lonely though," Susie said.

"Lonely?"

"Yeah, lonely. It's such an awful big house for just one little girl. I can already tell she's gonna want some people to play with."

"She told you that, I guess?"

"I can tell. And she's right. We have this big house and now you've got the good job. Would almost be a sin to not have a whole herd of little feet running around here."

"A herd?"

"Three sounds about right. All little girls. Real close together. What do you think?"

"Does it have to be here?" Jerry asked. "You ever thought about us leaving, moving out West somewhere? A new life?"

"A new life? Baby, we've got everything we want here."

"But what if things here aren't really what we want?"

"Why wouldn't they be? I know it's been a crazy few months, but things is about to settle down. I can feel it."

With her toes, Susie pulled the sheriff's shirt Jerry had dropped in the floor toward them. "I just love seeing you in this uniform."

She reached down and picked it up. She pulled it to her cheek to rub against her face. "I do love this shirt. People see that badge, and they know who's the most important man in Buckner County."

"I surely don't believe that's me."

"Well, I do."

He looked back to her and she caught his chin again. She pulled him to her and kissed him.

"Come on," she said, standing and reaching for his hand. "And get this stuff out of here. You aint sleeping in the parlor."

*   *   *

Jerry woke a few minutes before the bedside table's digital clock was set to go off at 4:15. He disabled the alarm, so it would not wake Susie. He lay there looking at the ceiling, the rays of moonlight slicing into his room. One beam bathed his wife in a soft bluish glow. He looked at her hair covering her pillow. Her naked back too. The porcelain skin captured the moonlight and shared it with Jerry, inviting his touch.

He swung his feet from the bed and covered Susie's back with his section of their down comforter. "I put you two biscuits in the microwave," she said, without opening her eyes. "Thirty seconds."

Jerry ate his breakfast as he drove to the fork in Troublesome Creek where he intended to hunt out of the beech tree he found with Andrew. He arrived and unloaded his gear: a large flashlight and another one to wear on his hat, two knives, gauze and tape to stop a bleed, and an elk call.

His last item was the Beretta. He took off his gloves to feel the cold steel and laminated maple and walnut stock. He smelled the metal and stained grain wood, as if it were a living being. It called to him, longing to be used.

When he saw the company's name etched in the barrel, he thought about the day when Big Dan gave him the rifle. He thought about the empty house, and the toast they made over beer. He thought about the blue quilt with the dogwood blooms. But mostly, he thought about Big Dan.

"Aw hell," Jerry said to himself. "Let's get this over with."

Jerry returned the gear and the rifle to his car and drove to Buckner County's protected section of the Daniel Boone National Forest. He found Big Dan's

SUV near a "No Hunting" warning and parked beside it. He collected his gear, the Beretta and put six .308 Winchester shells in his ammunition pouch, although he knew with the Beretta, he only needed one shot.

Jerry stood in front of Big Dan's SUV, trying to decide which way the old man would go for his hunt. Jerry knew Big Dan would want to have higher ground than the elk, and he decided a hill behind the parking lot was probably where Big Dan went. He took steps in that direction, and his hunch became certain. From atop that hill, Jerry heard a faint female elk call.

The squeaky whine of the elk cow was too high pitched for Jerry to believe originated from an animal in the wild. "Needs more growl," Jerry said to himself, as he began toward the sound. "He needs to work on that."

Jerry illuminated his hunting cap's flashlight, so Big Dan would not mistake him for a bull elk, bear or mountain lion and shoot him. Still thirty minutes before sunrise, Jerry only had that light from his cap and the wails and screeches from Big Dan to guide him. But they were enough. Each time Big Dan blew his call, Jerry heard the old man's imperfect plea to wayward bulls clearer and knew he was closer to his destination.

When Jerry approached the top of the mountain, he saw the silhouette of Big Dan, looking out over the other side. The old man put his hands over his mouth and made the call again, the shrill cry piercing through the subdued morning air. Jerry took another step toward Big Dan and cleared his throat. Big Dan whirled, with his rifle in his hands.

"Jerry, guess you came to check on me after all."

Jerry said nothing.

"I gotta take this call back to the gun shop," said Big

Dan, pulling the latex reed from his teeth. "They said this one would lure in a bull elk, but all it brought me was a sheriff."

Jerry reluctantly offered a slight chuckle as a reaction, conceding Big Dan had a wit like no other.

"Something on your mind, Jerry? Figured you'd be excited to be out this morning."

"Had a talk with Eddie yesterday."

"You talked to Eddie? What about?"

"He says that Andrew didn't do anything with Stanley Jennings. Wasn't connected to it at all."

"Did he say who he thought was involved?"

"Yeah."

"Who did he say?"

"Well, his son for one."

"Oh."

"And Steven."

"He said that?"

"Not in so many words, but yeah, Little Eddie and Steven killed Stanley. He told me."

"What else did he say?"

"That him and Danny let me think Andrew did it to keep them boys out of trouble."

"I see."

"You see?"

A sound from below Big Dan on the other side of the mountain interrupted their conversation. A bull elk bugled back to Big Dan's call from earlier. The piercing, sharp cry cut Jerry at the knees and caused him to crouch and hunker low to the ground.

"That's a big one," Big Dan whispered.

The bull grunted deep guttural growls. Big Dan placed his reed in his mouth and called back to the interested bull.

Jerry kept close to the ground and crept up to join Big Dan at the overlook. "You need to put more growl in that call," Jerry said. "Use more of your throat. Like you're snoring."

Big Dan nodded.

"You knew about all that, didn't you?" Jerry asked.

"Jerry, I don't know what to say. Nobody ever meant for things to turn out like they did. Just a bad break what happened with your brother, that's all."

"My nephew."

"Right, nephew. The boy had other problems, obviously."

The bull elk bugled again. His penetrating scream raised the hairs on Jerry's arm. The sausage biscuits Jerry ate earlier in the morning churned in his stomach and flooded his throat and mouth with salt and acid. Jerry struggled to swallow and focused on his breathing.

"He's gonna come right through there," Big Dan said and pointed to a break in the tree line that opened into the valley.

Jerry studied the layout and agreed with Big Dan's prediction.

"Well," said Big Dan, looking back to Jerry, "you aint shot me yet, so that's a good thing."

"You're really gonna try to joke about this?"

"Jerry, I don't know what to say."

"You lied to me," said Jerry. "Little Dan lied to me. Eddie basically lied to me. Until yesterday."

"We was just trying to protect our own," said Big Dan. "We thought you'd follow along. Everything was set for this to just go unsolved. Just go away."

"But I did my job?"

"Yeah. You did your job and did the right thing. You're a better person than all of us, Jerry. This proves it. And you know what that means?"

"What?"

"It means you're perfect to be leading the people of our county as our sheriff," said Big Dan.

"Are you patronizing me now?" asked Jerry. "Do you think I'm just some dumb hick?"

Big Dan's demeanor changed. The sales pitch and compassion disappeared from his voice. "Okay, enough of this," he said. "What's done is done. And I'm sorry. But it's up to you now, what you'll do with the truth now that you know it."

"I could call the State Police or the Feds," said Jerry.

"Absolutely. I can give you some numbers right now and you can call them from the top of this mountain. I bet you get good signal from up here." Big Dan reached a phone out for Jerry to take. "But what's that gonna do?"

"You could pay," said Jerry, as he stepped back from the phone and refused it.

"Justice?" asked Big Dan. "Is that gonna bring your nephew back? Or Eddie's boy? Or Stanley Jennings for that matter?"

"That's not what justice is about."

"You think I'm going to go to jail? Or any one of us?"

Jerry looked at Big Dan with confidence.

"Aw, come on now, Jerry. Me and you both know that aint gonna happen. Your word against ours?" Big Dan laughed. "If you go over my head, all you are going to do is run into prosecutors who will tell you that they love your story, but they don't have enough evidence to move forward."

Jerry said nothing.

"And then you'll be left with what? Because that nice

house you got now, you won't have it no more. And that nice job you got now, you won't have it no more neither."

"I can keep my job as sheriff if I keep getting elected," said Jerry.

Big Dan smiled at him and chuckled slightly. "Oh, Jerry. You're breaking my heart right now. Absolutely breaking my heart."

"I could win without you. I could."

"No, you couldn't. It don't work that way. Not in my county," Big Dan said. He turned his back to the valley, put his arm on Jerry's shoulder and looked into his sheriff's eyes with sincerity. "On the other hand, what if you don't call nobody? Despite what you might think, I like you, Jerry. There's times I ask myself why my boys can't be more like you. And despite your feelings for me at this very moment, I think we can still be good friends. It's awful good to be a friend of Big Dan's in Buckner County."

Jerry did not respond. He looked down from Big Dan's genuine eyes, unable to stomach the integrity the old man believed they conveyed. When he looked up, he saw movement in the valley below Big Dan. The elk trotted out from between a pair of hickory trees and galloped into the valley. It stopped in an overgrown field, grunting and snorting to a cow it believed had been calling all morning. The elk looked around, pawed at the browning fescue and crabgrass and turned his mouth to the sky to blast one more bugle that should bring his mysterious mate to him.

Big Dan turned back to the valley, as the first rays of morning sunshine showered the elk in the field. "Aint he a beauty?" he said of the copper brown body below them and admired the dark legs and burned auburn head and neck. The beast pranced and kicked in the field, trying to conjure an interested female.

Jerry counted the points. Each side had six for sure, maybe seven. And was that an eighth by the head? Yes, that's eight on each side that were undeniable points. He would have to measure the many bumps and spikes, but the animal clearly carried a rack of at least sixteen points.

"I see twenty-two," said Big Dan. "Twenty-two points. Never seen one like that before." He looked down at Jerry's Beretta and gave a nod with his head. Jerry looked back at Big Dan, confused. Was their conversation over? Is this how Big Dan wanted to end things?

"Go on, Jerry," Big Dan said. "He's yours. That's the biggest one in Buckner County, I bet. Maybe ever. Take him."

Big Dan reached down and lifted the Beretta toward Jerry's shoulder. Jerry stopped him.

"Go on," Big Dan whispered. "It's all right. We'll figure everything else out later. Just go ahead and get this elk."

Big Dan put a soft hand on Jerry's back. He patted it and held on to Jerry to pull him close.

"You're a fine man, Jerry Somerset," Big Dan said.

Jerry took off his right glove and retrieved a Winchester cartridge from his pouch. He slid it into the Beretta's chamber.

"There you go," Big Dan whispered.

Jerry pulled the gun to his body and nestled the stock just below the collarbone connected to his right shoulder. Through the Zeiss Victory telescopic sight, he studied the overgrown whiskers and the saliva dripping from the desperate, aroused male. Jerry found the heart and lung area on the body in the crosshairs, but the pool of water settling in Jerry's eye clouded his target and fogged the scope. Jerry blinked and released a single tear down his cheek. Fluid from his nose moistened his upper lip. With the camouflage glove on his left hand, Jerry wiped his eyes and nose. He found the elk again in his sight and took one last breath and held it. He tracked the elk in the scope, maintaining his target around the heart and lungs and waited for the elk to turn broadside to him and stop for an instant. The elk saw a small chestnut tree in the clearing below Jerry. It walked to the tree and began to pick at the leaves when Jerry squeezed the trigger.

*   *   *

"Hold on," Susie said. She grabbed a tissue and pretended to shine Jerry's badge. "So much better."

She kissed her husband.

"What are you gonna do today?" he asked.

"I guess I'll be looking up recipes for elk stew and elk casserole and elk parmesan."

Before walking to his car, Jerry stepped into the detached metal garage that he had commandeered as his exclusive work area. He popped on the fluorescent lights and heard them buzz as he looked over the giant elk suspended from the metal rafters by chains. Upside down, the elk's back feet were tethered to the center beam of the ceiling, and its front feet nearly extended to the cement floor below. The legs were positioned over galvanized tubs that collected blood. Pulled by gravity, the blood drained from the holes at the ends of the legs created when the hoofs were sawed off. Another tub collected blood draining from the elk's head. Jerry looked at the animal and counted the twenty points he considered legitimate. The last man to harvest a twenty-point elk in Buckner County may have been Daniel Boone himself. Jerry patted his prize's side and smoothed the waves in its hair.

Rather than occupying a seat at Sanderson's Café, Jerry decided this morning to get a donut and coffee at the Mountain Fishing, Hunting, Gardening and Hardware Store. Also a gas station. When he pulled into the parking lot, he looked up to see Jennifer walking out of the store with her son. The boy ran away from his mother and darted in front of a car. The driver slammed on the brakes to avoid him. Jennifer yelled at the boy and chased after him as he scurried between parked cars.

Jerry considered offering assistance, but he looked to the road and saw the blue Acura rocketing by the parking lot.

Jerry raced after the car and once again pulled over Bradley Donaldson.

"I didn't see you in court after all," said Jerry, as he approached the young man writing a ticket.

"Nope. I told ya. Taken care of," said Bradley.

"Your daddy had to pay a fine?" asked Jerry.

"I don't know. He just told me not to worry about it. And told me to tell you next time to go catch some bad guys."

"I see."

"So, you gonna give me another one? Waste everybody's time again?"

Jerry sighed and stopped writing the ticket. Jennifer's car passed on the road. As Jerry looked at her, she turned away.

"Ah hell, I guess not," said Jerry, returning his

attention to Bradley. "You been drinking? Or you got anybody tied up in the trunk?"

"No."

"Okay, then. Just slow it down a little bit though. There's some bad curves up through here. We get wrecks all the time. If you wanna stretch this car's legs, wait until you come over that hill near Troublesome Creek. Nice little straight stretch there. You can see what she's got."

"That's it?" said Bradley. "I can go?"

"Yeah, you can go."

Jerry stepped away from the car and watched Bradley spin and throw gravels off the shoulder and accelerate onto the road. He gunned his engine and fishtailed into the first curve he reached. Jerry walked back to his car and sat in the driver's seat for several minutes. He looked in the mirror and saw the reflection of his face and his badge. Jerry positioned the mirror so he could not see himself and drove away.

AUTHOR ACKNOWLEDGMENTS

Special thanks to Monica Sender for caring about my characters and helping me tell their story.

For research assistance, valuable information was provided by Mom & Dad and Hector Alcala.

Thank you to all the writers, editors and proofers who read this story in various forms and provided feedback, especially Alysia Grimm, Fady Hadid, Kat Gray, Lisa Franek and Daisy Sharrock.

Made in the USA
Coppell, TX
17 April 2020

20670551R00146